DEAD AND BUTTER

A Southern Psychic Sisters Mystery

A. GARDNER

To my little Sweet T & Sweet Pea

Dear Ms. Ember Greene,

According to our records, your
Seer license has expired. Please file
for a renewal with your regional
representative, and update your
current contact information.

Kind regards,
The Clairs

Dear Ms. Ember Greene,

According to our records, your Seer license has expired. Please file for a renewal with your regional representative, and update your current contact information.

Kind regards,
The Clairs

Chapter 1

The first time I fired someone, I felt sorry for the guy.

He hadn't been with the company long, and his wife had just found out she was pregnant. It took every ounce of energy I could muster to keep a straight face and refrain from telling him how sorry I was more than one time. I even concluded our meeting by convincing him to treat the situation as a valuable learning experience that would lead to something better.

I know. What a bunch of garbage.

After that, hiring and firing came easy. It was all part of the job. We all have families. We all have ups and downs in our personal lives. What my employees did on their own time was *their* business. And *my* business was to do whatever it took to land that big promotion.

"Do you understand, Erica? I don't care what did or didn't happen last night. Don't mix business with pleasure. Nothing good ever comes of that."

"All I said was that my boyfriend proposed," Erica repeated, raising a thick, penciled eyebrow. "Dang, Ms. Greene, they told me you go through assistants like fresh-brewed coffee, but I thought it was a joke."

"I just gave you some sound advice, and all you can think about is your morning latte? Perfect." I cleared my throat, hoping my new assistant would take the hint that it was time to leave. She didn't. "And get this letter off my desk. I told you to put letters from this particular address straight through the shredder."

"What's a Seer license anyway? Like a special driver's license?" Erica did her best to hide the wad of gum in her mouth when she talked. It didn't work. In fact, it was more distracting than the lime green beads on her necklace.

"You opened my mail?"

"You told me to check your messages." Erica shrugged as if her actions were justified. "Should I add the Clairs them to your contact list?"

"Definitely not."

Erica promptly left my office, but her questions lingered. The letters were becoming more and more frequent. At first, the messages had gone to my home address in Misty Key, Alabama. My mother called me every week to remind me. But the longer I went without replying to the Clairs, the more persistent they became. Now the letters were coming to New York City. They sounded like friendly reminders, but they weren't.

I shook the past from my mind and focused on the list of tasks on my screen, although my heart raced just thinking about the day I would have to do something about my expired Seer license. My eyes darted to a number on my desktop, and then another number, and then another. Finally, I looked at the time. My mother was currently dialing my work number. I swiftly informed Erica to hold all of my calls.

But moments later the phone in my office rang anyway. I knew it was Mom.

"So much for keeping my new assistant for longer than a week." I let the call go to voicemail. I already knew what my mother was going to say: the same things she said every time we spoke.

My sister Stevie was overwhelmed.

The bakery was extremely busy.

Carol Ann was looking for me again.

I always called her back in the evenings when I got home from work, and I knew that Mom knew that too.

My eyes darted to my computer screen again as a new email appeared in my inbox. The numbers practically jumped out at me as if they were doused in neon orange paint. This meant that they were trying to tell me something. I usually ignored them because the messages were never consistent, but this particular one appeared to be some sort of warning.

191. A particularly unlucky number in the world of aviation.

But I hadn't booked any flights recently.

Oh, no. Bryce. He's a pilot.

* * *

I ran my fingers through my shiny brown hair, a shade my sister referred to as caramel, one last time before Bryce arrived. He wasn't a fan of sushi, which was why we rarely visited my favorite restaurant. That didn't bother me because I had my usual spicy tuna rolls delivered to my apartment on Monday nights when he was normally out of town.

Bryce and I had been dating for two years, and we had the perfect relationship. I worked a lot, and he was gone all the time. We both had the freedom to focus on our careers, which made the times we did see each other more rewarding. Bryce understood that I'd been trying to snag a director position since I went to work for Fillmore Media. He didn't care that I wasn't at home sewing a new throw cushion and preparing nutritious home-cooked meals. I wasn't good at that stuff anyway. Since I'd moved away from home, Doris made all my meals.

Doris was what I called my microwave.

"Sorry I'm late." Bryce grinned as he sat across from me. He was still in his uniform—a getup that turned heads wherever he went. He would never admit it, but I knew he liked the added attention. I smiled as I pretended to read the menu.

"I ordered us appetizers."

"Of course you did," Bryce responded.

"How was Denver?"

"Denver?" Bryce glanced at the menu for fewer than five seconds. That meant one of two things: either he already knew what he wanted, or he wasn't planning on eating.

I couldn't stop myself from frowning.

"Your layover," I stated.

"Right." Bryce nodded, and I held up my menu, hinting that he should look over it one more time. He didn't.

A waiter approached the table and placed our appetizers in the center. I studied each plate and shook my head. I knew the kitchen would disregard my request for unsalted edamame. I heaved a sigh of annoyance.

"Excuse me, but I ordered this with *no* salt." I handed the appetizer back to the waiter. He apologized with a slight bow and headed back toward the kitchen.

"You can barely toast bread without burning it, and yet you're extra picky at restaurants." Bryce took a sip of water. His menu was facedown on the table now, and he'd even pushed it a few inches away.

"The settings on those things will forever remain a mystery to me," I argued. "I swear they design toasters these days just to drive me crazy."

"The bread burns because you ignore it."

"You should look over the menu again. I hope you're not going to order the same thing you did last time we came here, because you didn't like it, remember?"

"I said the bread burns because you ignore it," Bryce reiterated. "Kind of like this conversation."

A lump that was hard to swallow formed in my throat.

"You're not staying, are you?"

"No." Bryce leaned back in his chair and took a deep breath.

The numbers were right. Why are they always right?

"Okay, let's hear it." I pushed my menu aside and crossed my arms. I wiped the emotion from my face as was standard whenever I had to let someone go at work. It was better than tearing up. "Is there someone else?"

"Yes." Bryce didn't hesitate to answer. "There has been for quite some time." I studied the look on his face. He didn't seem nervous, afraid, or even remorseful. It was like he'd already moved on from *us*.

So why was this all new to me?

"You have got to be kidding me." I rolled my eyes, breaking my rule of remaining expressionless throughout the entire discussion. I couldn't help it. I wasn't prepared. "How long, Bryce?"

"Four months."

"*Four months?*" I said, raising my voice. "Wow, another unlucky number. I suppose next you'll be telling me the two of you are engaged or something."

"Ember, it's normal for you to be upset with me, but it's not like it's a secret. I've tried to tell you this multiple times." Bryce took another breath. "You never listen."

"Are you insinuating that I'm some kind of selfish prick? Because you know I'm not like that at all."

"We both want very different things," Bryce replied. "You're all about work, and there's nothing wrong with that. But I need someone who won't ignore my calls during work hours."

"My mother called you again, didn't she?" I was hoping that it wasn't true.

"No. But you shouldn't ignore her calls. She's your mom."

"I don't ignore her calls, and that's none of your business."

"Maybe if it *were* my business, we wouldn't be having this conversation."

"Just leave." I turned my head. My emotions swam in my head and my ability to stay calm and collected slowly slipped away. "And for the record, I heard you this time."

Bryce stood up.

"Well then, for the record, it didn't have to end this way." Bryce paused as the waiter returned with a new plate of edamame, minus the salt. I stared at the food with a sour stomach. Dining alone after breaking up with my boyfriend of two years was the last thing I needed.

"Your point being?"

"I sincerely hope you figure yourself out." Bryce nodded and walked past me for the last time.

He wasn't the first person to say something like that to me. I tended to keep my family as private as possible. I never told Bryce about me or my sisters and our special abilities. I never told him about the night I left Misty Key right after my dad died. I honestly thought that I could start a new life without all those memories. I never thought they would haunt me the way they did.

But numbers still speak to me somehow.

The crowded sushi joint suddenly felt empty—like I was the only person present in the entire restaurant. If I didn't see my own breakup coming, then what else in my life was I not seeing? I glanced down at my purse. Maybe this was what

Mom had been calling to tell me. I was certain that she already knew about Bryce and me.

I pulled out my wallet to pay for the appetizers.

Just as I did, my phone rang. It was a number I didn't recognize, and an Alabama area code. I raised my eyebrows and carefully answered it.

"Hello, I'm looking for Ember Greene." The man's stern voice pierced my chest like an icicle.

"Yes, this is she," I replied. "Can I help you?"

"This is Detective Winter with the Misty Key Police Department," the man continued. "You're a hard woman to get ahold of, Ms. Greene."

"I'm sorry, is there a problem, Detective?"

"I need to ask you a few questions about your little sister."

"Aqua?" I instinctively gripped the phone tighter as the face of my baby sister flashed before my eyes, along with the promise I made her right before I moved to New York. "Why? What's wrong? What's happened?"

"My apologies, ma'am. I thought you knew."

"Knew what?"

"Your sister is missing." He paused for a few seconds.

"How long?" I closed my eyes, ready for the answer.

I knew the number that was running through his brain.

"*Four* days."

Chapter 2

"So, I get today off?" Erica looked up from her laptop with a smirk.

"Just because I'm going out of town, that doesn't mean you get an early Friday," I clarified. "I'll be back first thing Monday, and there's plenty of work to do." I skimmed through my email list, talking through the upcoming discussion I would be having with my boss. Leaving during a big project was a bad idea, but my hands were tied. My family needed me, and I couldn't ignore it.

"Oh, should I get that?" Erica asked when the phone rang.

"Yeah, you should."

"Right, okay." Erica answered the phone on my desk. "Fillmore Media, Ember Greene's office. Uh-huh. Uh-huh. Okay." Erica held out the receiver. "It's your mom. She told me to tell you that if you don't leave in twenty minutes, you'll miss your flight."

I took the phone from Erica.

"Yes, Mom, thank you for that advice," I said. "But I do have a few hours before my flight, so I'm sure I'll be fine."

"There will be more traffic than usual," my mother responded in her usual tone. It took me back to my teens when she'd insisted on giving me details about every one of the boys I dated. Most of it was stuff I didn't want to know. "I had a dream last night."

"Okay, I'll leave as soon as I can," I agreed.

"Don't say that just to shut me up. You really should leave early, pumpkin."

"I will," I insisted, dismissing Erica with a wave. This time, Erica took the hint and left my office. I took a deep breath and cleared my head. Or tried to. I hadn't been able to sleep at all since Detective Winter's phone call, and my mother had insisted that the details of Aqua's disappearance were better off spoken in person. "Any more news this morning?"

"The police patrolled all night," she answered. "They haven't found any new leads."

"I just don't understand." My vision blurred for a moment. I let tears form in the corners of my eyes before dabbing away the moisture. I didn't want to look like a hurricane of emotions when my boss came by. "Someone at the Crystal Grande *must* know something."

"Honey, we deliver to them every week. Half the time, those kitchen employees don't even check to make sure all of the bread and breakfast pastries are accounted for. It doesn't surprise me that no one seems to remember what Aqua was up to that morning."

"And you're sure that detective guy knows what he's doing?" I continued.

"You're getting worked up again." She paused. "There's not much we can do until you get here, okay?"

"And Stevie?" I hadn't spoken to my older sister in over three years. Not because I didn't want to speak with her. Stevie made it clear when I moved away that she was no longer a part of my life. I still sent my little ten-year-old nephew, Orion, the occasional care package—books and trinkets mostly. He was just about my only real friend still left in Misty Key besides the family dog.

"Stevana has assured me that everything is fine," Mom stated.

"So, she hasn't—"

"No." Mom's reply was immediate. "No. She hasn't seen Aqua. And if she had, she would have told me right away."

"Good." I gulped.

My older sister, Stevie, was a medium. So, for her, seeing my sister would have meant only one thing—that Aqua was dead.

A knock interrupted my thoughts. My heart pounded as I glanced at the doorway, ready to tell Erica that I was still on the phone. It was my boss, Mr. Cohen. He was a man of few words, which was refreshing at sometimes and scary as hell at others. On the one hand, meetings were brief and straight to the point. But on the other, I never knew exactly where I stood.

"Am I interrupting something important?" Mr. Cohen asked, tilting his head the way he usually did when waiting for a response.

"No, sir," I answered.

"Oh, the big boss," Mom whispered into the phone as if she were in my office with me. "My chances of an *I love you* are long gone."

"I'll see you tonight," I told her before hanging up.

"Nice job with the Tinley account," Mr. Cohen said, making himself comfortable in the nearest chair. His eyes darted around my office, stopping at every knickknack as if it gave away my inner thoughts. I doubted my monogrammed pencil cup told him much. "You do have a way with numbers."

"Thank you."

"It's a shame you'll be gone for the weekend. We could really use your help with the new budget." His nostrils flared. He was holding back the rest of his comment.

"The budget will still be here when I get back," I stated as confidently as I could.

"Yes, it will."

"And I'll be here next week when Mr. Fillmore is in town." I nodded. It was the day I'd been preparing for all year. The day the owner of the company would appoint a new Director of Finance. That position had my name all over it, according to the numbers. I'd made the most effort. I'd saved the company hundreds of thousands of dollars on more than one occasion, and nobody put in as many hours as I did.

"Ah, yes. The big meeting. You won't want to miss that." Mr. Cohen cleared his throat, placing a hand on the beer gut that seemed to be more and more swollen every time I saw him. The same went for the gray in his hair. He'd been a solid brunette when I was first hired three years ago.

"I'll be working as much as I can while I'm gone," I added. "I promise, it'll be like I never left."

"Where is it you're going again?" He narrowed his eyes.

"Home," I answered.

"Which is where?"

"Alabama."

The corner of his lip twitched. He leaned forward, making the roundness of his belly much more prominent. "Alabama? Are there roads and running water down there? I'll bet it was a surprise to see that we city folk wear shoes every day." He chuckled at his own brashness.

I forced a smile to be polite. No matter where I went, southern stereotypes still followed me. I hated it. Yet another reason why I worked hard to keep my private life a mystery to most of my coworkers. Some of them knew about Bryce, but none of them knew his name or how long we'd been dating. Or that we'd broken up.

"Good one. I certainly have never heard that one before."

"Well, good luck, Ember. I hope you have a nice visit."

"Me too," I replied.

* * *

Touching down in Mobile, Alabama, brought back more memories than I was ready for. Most of them were of my dad and the times we'd people-watched at the airport before boarding a flight. He'd insisted on a family vacation every summer. Some of them were more lavish than others. It all depended on how well the bakery was doing. Dad was a number cruncher, although he didn't see numbers the way I did.

Maybe if he had, he would still be alive.

The heat was immediate, even though it was fall. The leaves up north were turning brilliant shades of orange, red, and yellow. But in the south, it was either green or *not* green. The humidity brushed against my skin as I stepped outside to find my rental car. It was a long drive toward the coast. Long enough for me to do some breathing exercises and repeat a few calming affirmations to myself.

I had no idea what to expect, or the state in which I would soon find my mother.

She'd sounded just fine on the phone, but I knew that she had been crying herself to sleep at night, wondering what had happened to her little girl and pleading to the universe to send her a prophetic dream about Aqua's whereabouts.

My windows fogged as I messed with the air conditioner. The familiar scent of must wafted through the car as cool air blasted through the vents. The product of too much moisture, it created a smell that reminded me of moldy fruit. But after a couple of days, I would get used to it.

My jaw clenched when I saw the road sign for Misty Key. I would be arriving just in time for dinner. Stevie would have just closed the bakery and Mom was most likely serving her usual sweet chicken salad sandwiches with whatever bread was leftover from the day. They were better than anything I could cook. My time had been best spent in the office with Dad. Stevie took care of the books now in addition to being Head Baker.

As the evening approached, the sky turned gray, and the wind grazed along the coast like it did before it rained. The highway took me along the shoreline, where I saw the waves of the gulf rolling alongside me. It was a peaceful sight—one I wished could stay that way. The highway went straight into town where the Crystal Grande Hotel stood like a beacon to passing tourists. Misty Key was a beach town, which meant that Main Street was filled with souvenir shops and ice cream carts.

And, of course, Lunar Bakery.

My family didn't live far from the bakery. It was within walking distance from the house. Dad had often gone for long walks and ended up having his evening sweet tea in the peace and quiet of the darkened kitchen. He always took Yogi with him— hunting, boating, or working, his red bloodhound had been at his side.

A droplet hit the windshield and then another. Within minutes, it was pouring. The south was funny that way. When summer hit, it was greener than an orchard of peach trees. But when it rained, it poured. It poured so much that a small pond formed in the center of Misty Key Square. When we were kids, Stevie and I would go there in search of toads.

I slowed down as I passed the bakery.

The lights were off, and the sign out front displayed the special of the week—*Good Vibes Vanilla Cake*. It was Stevie's invention. Only she would think to pair herbs from the garden with vanilla beans. I glanced in the mirror and realized I was smiling. Misty Key was the keeper of a happy childhood. But it also harbored the guilt I struggled with every time I looked in the mirror.

Seeing Main Street at dinnertime made the guilt so much worse.

My mother waved as I pulled into the driveway. Yogi waited next to her, his tail wagging and his tongue catching drops of rain. I took a deep breath as I parked and grabbed my purse that was nestled comfortably in the front seat. Mom didn't care about the rain and ran to hug me.

"Come on in," she said. "Dinner is on the table." She grabbed my bag and hurried inside the house. Yogi waited, looking up at me as I hesitated to move.

"Hey, boy," I said quietly, wiping a strand of wet hair from my face. "How bad is it in there?"

Yogi barked, one short, curt bark.

"That bad, huh?"

My childhood home reminded me of the little beach cottages for rent along the coastline. It sat on stilts high enough to park your car underneath, as did all the other houses in our neighborhood, and a palm tree graced the front entrance. Long porches stretched along both sides of the house, and the color of the door changed with Mom's mood. When I was a kid, the door was normally lemon yellow. Today it was blue. A deep *aqua* blue.

I walked inside to a cozy family room complete with decorative pillows, woolen blankets, and a collection of candles sitting on the mantelpiece. Yogi wiped his paws and led me upstairs, where my mom had placed my suitcase in my old room. My stomach went sour when I saw a stack of envelopes on the bed.

"I thought you would want to get changed before you eat," Mom suggested. She wore a thick navy sweater, even though it was warm outside. Her light brown hair was tied up in a bun, revealing chestnut eyes to match. They were sunken with a ring of puffiness around the edges.

"Mom, are you okay?"

"I have hope," she replied.

I grabbed her arm and squeezed the bulky layer of clothing.

"You've been eating properly and taking your pills, right?"

"Oh, you sound just like those society ladies." She frowned and dismissed my comment.

"You're *still* part of the Misty Key Women's Society? I thought you quit after Dad died."

"I'm back again," she informed me. "And yes, the ladies are just as gabby and judgmental as before. I love it." She played with her necklace, a dainty silver chain with a small moonstone. Sometimes she teased that she would leave it to the daughter she liked best when she died. It was her way of coaxing us to always stay on her good side.

"How is the bakery?"

"Your sister is doing a great job, but she could always use help," she responded, raising her eyebrows. "You'll have to look through the books while you're in town."

"If Stevie will let me," I replied, taking a deep breath and brushing aside the stack of letters on my bed. I set my purse down in front of them. I would throw those letters in the trash too, once Mom left the room.

"You can't hide from them forever." She eyed the pile of letters I'd attempted to cover.

"Who says I'm hiding?" I lifted my chin, trying to appear as if the frequent notices to renew my Seer license were no big deal. "I have other priorities right now, and dinking around with cosmic rays or whatever is not one of them."

"I see." My mother glanced at me, but she did it in a special way. It was like she saw right through me. And she probably did. Her eyes darted around the room—from the cross-stitched pillow of a star constellation on my bed to the framed picture on my wall of my dad and me at my high school graduation.

"What, no lecture?" My heart raced, and my stomach churned with all of the arguments we'd had about me wasting my future. "No talk about how I'm wasting my thirties? No stories about how numerology is a rare talent that I should celebrate? No side tangents about how the Clairs have stopped wars and saved numerous souls?"

"I don't have to lecture you," Mom commented. "You do that all on your own."

"Well, I don't intend on renewing my Seer license. I just want to make that clear. I know the consequences, and I'm prepared to deal with them."

"You would ruin centuries of tradition for a desk job in New York City?" My mom tugged at her moonstone some more. If she were to die tomorrow, that sparkling gem on her chest would definitely not be left to me.

"It's more than a desk job. Listen, Mom, I don't want to argue with you. I've had a very stressful week, and I just want to focus on finding Aqua." I straightened my blouse, finally ready to face my big sister who was downstairs at the kitchen table. No doubt Stevie had a long list of accusations prepared just for the occasion.

"Oh, yes." She briefly hung her head and sighed. "You and Bryce."

"I don't need to tell you what happened, then."

"Nope." She shook her head.

Part of me was annoyed that she knew so much about my personal life. But the other part of me was relieved that I didn't have to talk about it. Mom already knew everything there was to know and I wouldn't be forced to retell my breakup story over and over again so she could analyze it.

"Good." I headed for the door. "As you would say, Bryce and I just weren't meant to be."

"As long as you're okay."

"I'm great," I lied, although Bryce's betrayal still stung. I'd never felt as blindsided as I had when we'd split up. I'd also lost my appetite for sushi thanks to him. "Breaking up with Bryce was for the best."

"I'm glad you have it all figured out."

My nostrils flared. I knew there was more sarcasm to her comment than truth.

"I do."

"Let's eat then." She tilted her head toward the staircase. "You must be hungry after such a long drive."

I wasn't.

If anything, the long drive had given me time to come up with plenty of reasons to refrain from entering the kitchen altogether. The number one reason being my sister Stevie.

Chapter 3

Like the rest of the house, the kitchen looked the
same. Natural lighting was important to Mom,
which was why she'd insisted on installing two
skylights above the sink and the kitchen table.
Sitting down to a meal felt like sitting outside. The
white cabinets and the collection of crystals on the
counter added to the serene ambience. The rain
pattered outside and provided the perfect amount of
white noise to drown out the sound of clanging
silverware and Yogi's constant whining for his next
scrap.

Mom sat at her usual end of the table as she
scooped another helping of sweet chicken salad
onto her grandson's plate. Orion accepted the extra
serving, setting down his latest comic book and
eagerly biting into the day-old bread. Yogi wagged
his tail as I lifted my sandwich toward my mouth.
He hadn't left my side, and I wasn't sure if it was
because he'd missed me or he thought I was a messy
eater.

Stevie hardly touched her food as she surfed
through emails on her phone. So far a mere glance
was the only communication I'd received from her.
It was better than a slap in the face. Stevie looked
just as I remembered her, with her jet-black hair

and a sleeve of tattoos that represented her star sign. Being the eldest, she'd been named after my dad, Steven, but the two of them couldn't be more different. My dad had been a conservative, God-fearing, sensible man and Stevie had a hard time saving curse words for when customers weren't around. She also had my mother's gift for baking, which was why Lunar Bakery was still in business.

"Sweetheart, eat something," my mother urged her. "I added more sugar and sweet pickle relish just the way you like it."

"I don't have much of an appetite this evening," Stevie responded in her usual tone. The way she glared at people as she spoke came across as intimidating to everyone who didn't know her. But really, it was her way of concentrating on one soul at a time. Being a medium meant that she was constantly distracted with inquiries from both the living and the dead.

"I guess Orion and I are the only ones interested in these leftover cheddar croissants?" Mom passed the platter toward me, studying my plate. I'd taken a couple of bites of my dinner, but that was about it.

"I ate on the plane." I blurted out the excuse before I could think of a better one. My eyes darted to the food in the center of the table and a copy of the day's local newspaper. I cringed when I came face-to-face with the *Misty Messenger*. It brought back a slew of unwanted memories that made me even more anxious and eager to escape to the privacy of my own bedroom.

"You're lucky to be alive," Orion stated, his bright blue eyes leering in my direction. His hair was jet-black like Stevie's, but the origins of his eye color remained a mystery—much like the identity of his father. "A lady died once from a bite of poisoned shrimp. Her insides melted and came oozing out through her ears."

"Where did you read that?" Stevie scolded him. "You know how I feel about you surfing the web when I'm not around."

"*Strange Ways to Die*," Orion proudly responded. His cheekiness matched that of his mother. "Auntie Ember gave it to me last Christmas."

"That's right. I did." I nodded in agreement, pursing my lips together as Orion gave a mischievous grin.

"Oh, I just love the shrimp they serve down at The Steamer," my mom said. "Your pop and I spent one too many anniversaries there drinking our fair share of mint juleps."

It wasn't unusual for her to litter a conversation with potholes.

"I could use a mint julep right about now," Stevie muttered under her breath.

"There's also an entire chapter on black death," Orion continued. "Speaking of which—"

"Yes, we all know that you want to be a plague doctor for Halloween," Stevie interrupted. "But remember what happened last year?"

"Fine." Orion rolled his eyes. "But how was I supposed to know that Becky Grimen had never heard of the Ebola virus, or the signs and symptoms exhibited by patient zero?"

"You're ten years old," Stevie pointed out. "Let's focus on the lighter side of Halloween."

"You mean the candy?"

"Sure." Stevie clenched her jaw as she sat up straighter.

"Auntie Ember," Orion went on. "Do you want to see my pet tarantula? Yogi almost ate her once." Orion raised his eyebrows and smiled again. I smiled too, glad that at least one member of my family wasn't put off by my presence.

"I'm sure your aunt has better things to do," Stevie said. She turned toward me, observing my choice of attire. I was wearing a black pencil skirt and matching blouse, which clashed with her after-hours uniform of a tank top and jean shorts. When winter approached, she would switch out her tank top for a shirt with sleeves.

"I would love to see your room, Orion."

"Yes," he murmured with excitement.

"Finish your dinner first," Stevie insisted.

A few moments of silence passed as we all picked at our food. Yogi gave up on begging for scraps and sat quietly at my feet. Stevie looked at her phone some more, and Orion flipped through the pages of his comic book as he tried to finish his food. My mom stared out the window at the pouring rain. The palm trees in the yard swayed back and forth, and gray clouds continued to roll in and block the last bit of sunshine for the day.

My mom gulped as she tugged at her moonstone.

"I had a dream last night," she breathed.

Stevie immediately looked up.

"You know where Aqua is?" Stevie leaned forward.

"I was waiting until we were all together," my mom explained. "It is important that we all discuss this as a family."

"Is she alive?" I asked, my chest tightening with every passing second.

"Yes, but her time is scarce." She took a moment to steady her breathing as a tear formed in her eye. "She's somewhere dark. She's confused. And there was a clock."

"A clock?" Stevie repeated.

"Yes." She dabbed at the corner of her eye. "That means that she won't be alive for long. We have to find her before it's too late."

"Oh, thank the stars," Stevie muttered. "I knew she couldn't have just eloped like the police think she did. Aqua would *never* do something like that without telling me."

"So, you think she was abducted?" I questioned my mother.

"I *know* it." She clasped her hands together to stop them from shaking. "There was nothing unusual about the morning she went missing. She got ready to make her usual trip to Crystal Grande Hotel to deliver bread. She fed Yogi. She had weekend plans with Rickiah. And then, she just never came home."

"And the self-centered pricks at the hotel claim nothing unusual happened that morning," Stevie added.

"Her crest reading with Lady Deja is scheduled for next month." Mom sniffled. "She was so excited to get her Seer license and start working for the Clairs." Her sniffles gave way to sobs.

Stevie jumped from her seat and wrapped an arm around her. My heart sank as I saw the pained look on my mother's face. I didn't know what it felt like to lose a child, but I imagined that it was close to some of the darkest feelings I'd ever felt in my own life. I walked to the other side of the table to offer a hug, but Stevie stuck out a hand.

"Stop right there," Stevie stated, addressing me directly for the very first time. "Your services are not needed."

"Excuse me?"

"We manage just fine without you around here and today is no different." Stevie's eyes narrowed as she shot me a foreboding glare.

"She's my mother too," I argued.

"She's *my mother* too," Stevie mocked. "Do you hear yourself? You don't even sound like a southerner anymore. You dress like the receptionist at the Crystal Grande, and you hardly smile. You've erased all traces of Misty Key from your life, and now you expect us to behave like you never left." Her pale cheeks turned a shade of crimson.

"If this is about the bakery then just say so," I responded.

"It's more than that, and you know it."

Yogi leaped up on all fours, and Orion looked from me to his mom.

I knew coming home would present me with a list of new problems that I didn't need on my plate at the moment. I was grateful that Stevie had gotten to the meat of her issues with me, but I was frustrated by the fact that she refused to put herself in my shoes. She had no idea what life was like outside of Misty Key, and she couldn't blame me for leaving her to run the family business all by herself if she never asked for help.

But still, a thought stirred in my chest. I couldn't stand the way Stevie looked at me. It was as if she knew my secret. It was as if she knew why I *really* left Misty Key years ago. If she did, I would lose her too.

Yogi's sudden bark cut through the tension in the room.

A noise tapped at the back of my head, and Yogi wasted no time trotting to the front door as another knock sounded through the hallway. Mom wiped her cheeks and forced a smile as she stood up. Stevie eyed her earnestly, as if she might faint at any minute. She held out her arms, offering a convenient crutch. "Not so fast," Stevie said. "Let me get the door, Ma."

"No, I need to get up and walk around." She glanced out the window at the darkening sky. "Though I don't know who would be calling at this hour in the middle of a storm."

"Carol Ann," Stevie confessed. Her gaze shifted in my direction as my lungs practically froze. Carol Ann worked as our regional representative for the Clairs. She'd been trying to get in touch with me ever since my Seer license had expired.

"And how long did you wait to call her after you found out that I'd be visiting?" I tilted my head, expecting no less from her.

"I submitted a request that the Clairs investigate Aqua's disappearance," Stevie corrected me.

"Oh." I placed a hand on my chest.

"Well, we need all the help we can get." Mom walked carefully to the front door.

My eyes darted to various spots around the kitchen. I wasn't sure what to do. Carol Ann would surely bombard me with questions. It'd been easy to ignore the letters, but I couldn't ignore Carol Ann in person. I took a deep breath and ran through a list of excuses in my head—anything I could say to buy me some time before I was forced to comply or lose something I could never get back.

"So many rules," Orion muttered, finishing his last bite of sweet chicken salad. "That's what Mom says. The only reason she follows them is because she gets to help people."

"There's a lot more to it than that," I added as I bit the corner of my lip.

The sound of voices filled the hall as Stevie and my mom greeted their guest. My heart pounded, and I tried not to look toward the entrance to the kitchen.

"Don't the Clairs help people?" Orion asked, wrinkling his nose in confusion.

"Yes, but—"

"Then why don't you want to help them anymore?" He scratched his head and squinted in my direction.

I remembered my early impressions of the Clairs when I was a little girl. I was taught that anyone born with a special ability had a duty to help others, and I aspired to be just like Lady Deja one day. Orion was right. The Clairs were a psychic organization that had the heavy responsibility of keeping the peace between magical species. Humans weren't the only ones who roamed the planet. And being born with a psychic gift meant that my intuition always led me to the heart of any conflict.

My grandmother and my mother saw things through prophetic dreams, and Stevie could communicate with the dead. Aqua's talents would be clearer once she had her crest reading with Lady Deja, and Orion's gift, if he had one, wouldn't show up until puberty.

It had been a Greene family tradition to work for the Clairs as mediators and peacemakers. Once a contract was signed and a Seer license was issued, a psychic was given assignments on a case-by-case basis. There was only one way to break a contract, and that meant agreeing to give up the special piece of your soul that you were born with—your psychic chi.

"I do." I took a deep breath. "But sometimes when a person tries to help, they do more harm than good."

"Right through here," Stevie said as she escorted a woman into the kitchen and offered her a seat at the table.

I narrowed my eyes, remembering Carol Ann to be much older and brunette.

"It smells like a bakery in here," the woman commented. She scanned the rest of the kitchen. "Are those cheddar croissants I smell?"

"Why, yes," my mother replied. She offered her the plate of them. "Please, have one."

"Thank you, Leila." The woman studied each croissant before choosing one. When she finally did, she took a tiny bite before directing her attention at me.

"You must be Ember," the woman said. "I see you're finally paying a visit to Misty Key. Tell me, is New York City all that you hoped it would be?"

"I'm sorry, *who* are you?"

"Don't be so rude," Stevie muttered.

"My name is Nova, your new regional representative." The woman held out her hand. Her auburn hair glistened a fierce red under the lights in the kitchen, and her face was smooth compared to the seasoned wrinkles I'd been used to seeing when Carol Ann came for a visit.

"What happened to Carol Ann?" I asked.

"She retired," Nova responded. "Believe me, it was about time. She was way too lax with all of the psychics in this area." Nova's gaze fell to me and only me. "For one, she let you slip under the radar time and time again with an expired Seer license." Nova reached into the dark leather messenger bag on her shoulder and pulled out a thick folder of papers. She handed them to me, and I cautiously accepted.

"A simple renewal form?" I said with a hint of sarcasm.

"It has been a while," Nova explained. "Most everything in your file needs updating." Her twisted half-smile made me uneasy. Nova was going to be a tricky one to deal with. And as she raised her eyebrows when I set the folder on the kitchen table, I realized that I'd taken Carol Ann for granted most of my life. At least Carol Ann had seen me as a person and not another number—an outlier that needed fixing so the data would line up just right.

"Nevermind her," Stevie interrupted, placing a hand on Mom's shoulder. "What about the request I submitted? The police department has been no help."

"Yes, your request has been processed." Nova paused and scratched the tip of her pointed nose. It was the sharpest feature on her otherwise full face. "Unfortunately, we're short-staffed. None of the

Seers that could help with this sort of thing are available."

"What?" Stevie rolled her eyes, out of patience and hospitality. She crossed her arms and bit the inside of her lip as she forced herself to take a deep breath. "My sister is missing. I think our case should be made a priority."

"Well—"

"Ma, tell her about your dream," Stevie insisted.

"You had a vision, Leila?" Nova questioned her.

"It's true." My mom cleared her throat as she squeezed the moonstone hanging from her neck. "My little girl is in trouble and her time is short. Action must be immediate, or she might not make it."

"I see," Nova replied, glancing down at her sensible tennis shoes. "The only thing I can do is request that your case is given top priority."

"Can't we just speak with Lady Deja?" Stevie's eyes widened, as did Nova's.

"Lady Deja and her council have other things to worry about,. You don't become Head Clair without having a tight schedule every waking moment. She is far too busy. No. I will see what I can do for you folks." She tilted her head toward the folder on the table. "In the meantime, please fill those forms out, Ember."

Yogi barked as Nova took one last sniff of her cheddar croissant and then set it down on the table. Orion looked up at her with a wrinkled nose. He opened his mouth to say something, but Stevie stopped him with one of her foreboding glares.

"Do let us know the moment you hear anything," Mom said as she escorted Nova out of the kitchen.

"I absolutely will."

When the front door slammed shut, Mom sulked back into the kitchen.

"Carol Ann always brought caramels," Orion stated. "Why didn't Nova bring me candy?"

"Those were pralines," Stevie corrected him, "and Nova is nothing like Carol Ann." Stevie rolled her eyes. "For one, her pet Siamese follows her everywhere. That stupid thing practically gave me the evil eye the entire time she was here. Yogi even barked at it."

"I didn't see a cat anywhere," Mom said..

"It's dead." Stevie's nostrils flared as she clenched her jaw. "First that detective, and now the Clairs. Screw them all. I'm finding Aqua myself."

"Me too," I added. My mind reflected back on the thing I'd said to my little sister right before I took a job in New York. I told her that I would always be there for her since my father no longer could. It was a promise I hadn't kept, and it killed me inside.

"You?" Stevie smirked. "When was the last time you even used your gift?"

"It shows up every once in a while," I confessed.

"Fine." Stevie patted Orion on the head as he stood up. "Meet me at the bakery in one hour."

"Oh, I want to come too," Orion whined.

"No, you're off to bed."

"Rats," Orion muttered.

"Now, honey, this isn't the time to push your sister away." Mom looked from Stevie and then to me. "You two need to figure out how to get along, for Aqua's sake."

"Oh, I have a plan." Stevie lifted her chin matter-of-factly. "Revenge is something I've put aside for the time being."

"Lucky me," I commented.

"*For Aqua's sake*," Stevie added.

Chapter 4

Entering the Lunar Bakery was for me like stepping into a time capsule. The café was dark, but it didn't matter. The same familiar smell of fresh bread and pastries hit me when I walked through the door. The counter at the front housed the same register and display case of Stevie's latest cake creations. The wood floors and peach-colored walls reminded me of every other sweet little tourist shop on Main Street, minus the star constellations painted on the ceiling. My mother had done those back when the bakery first opened. The gold paint was subtle but still edgy enough to give the place a unique twist.

"I see nothing has changed," I said. Stevie turned the lights on in the kitchen, and I rolled up my sleeves, grateful that I'd changed into yoga pants but regretting I'd grabbed a long-sleeved T-shirt to match. Even though the sun had gone down and most of the shops were closed, it was still hotter than I was used to.

"Don't you own anything with color anymore?" Stevie remained in her shorts and tank top as she scanned everything in the fridge and pantry.

"These pants are comfortable," I argued, glancing down at my black and gray attire. "And they were expensive."

"I normally prep for the next day after Orion goes to bed." Stevie continued with her work. "There was an incident last year involving Yogi, pounds of flour, and a wedding cake gone horribly wrong. I'll never let this place lose that much business ever again."

"I see you're still inventing new flavors," I said, remembering the sign I'd seen when driving through Misty Key. "Good vibes vanilla cake?"

"Customers love a good theme," Stevie admitted. "We're not called *Lunar* Bakery for no reason." She pulled out a clipboard and reviewed each item on her list. "Shooting stars, I forgot that I have two specialty cupcake orders tomorrow."

"So business is steady then?"

"It's steady even without Pops here to handle the books." She avoided eye contact, and I knew why. Handling the numbers was supposed to be my job. "I make it work. Despite what you may think, I'm much smarter than I look."

I sighed. Stevie's underhanded comments weren't something I had time for.

"It's late." I glanced at my watch. "Let's talk about Aqua."

"I appreciate your concern, but the only reason I asked you here was to keep Ma from having a heart attack." Stevie continued to busy herself with random tasks. Anything to keep herself from having to look at me.

"I can't force you to like me, Stevie, but we're still related. I'm going to do whatever I can to find Aqua, whether you like it or not. It would make your life easier if you just filled me in on everything that's been going on." Something buzzed in my pocket. I pulled out my cell phone to see that I had a new email from my boss. The subject line read *Weekend meeting notice*. Attached was an agenda.

"Missing your shiny office in NYC?" Stevie murmured, chuckling to herself.

I bit the corner of my cheeks and took a deep breath. *Family* was the only thing I continuously failed at. Getting on a plane bound for Mobile, Alabama, had taken a lot of courage. Renting a car and driving to Misty Key had been even more nerve-wracking. The only thing keeping me going were my memories of Aqua and the times she'd come to me for advice. I'd promised her I'd always be there for her.

Now was my chance to keep that promise despite the mistakes I'd made in the past.

"Here." To prove a point, I slid my phone across the counter. "If this is what it'll take to show you I'm serious, here. Take it."

Stevie paused, glancing at the phone as the screen lit up again notifying me of another email.

Stevie took a deep breath and looked me square in the eyes for the second time that evening. Her eyes never softened, but her permanent scowl disappeared as she slid the phone back to me.

"Fine." She cleared her throat and tilted her head toward a pair of stools in the corner. I followed her as she sat down. "I'll tell you what you want to know. But first, you have to promise me something."

"Name it."

"Once we start digging, you can't leave until we've found some answers," Stevie replied. "You have no idea how hard it was for Ma around here after Pops died. She got even worse when you took that job up north and left me to run the bakery by myself."

"Listen, I—"

"I don't want any explanations," Stevie continued, holding up a hand. "I just want your word that you won't give Mom another reason to lie awake crying at night."

I put my phone back in my pocket as it buzzed again. I would have to respond to my emails while Stevie was asleep. I could manage both. I mean, Stevie had to sleep sometime, and I was used to running on little shut-eye and liters of coffee.

"I'm also much smarter than I look." I stuck my hand out in agreement. Stevie shook it with a suspicious look on her face. "What's your plan?"

"The police aren't doing much," Stevie explained. "They say Aqua most likely ran away and will contact someone when she's ready, but Ma and I both know that is completely ludicrous. I think whatever happened to her has to do with the Crystal Grande Hotel. I've been getting a funny vibe from that place lately."

"So, you want to ask questions and do some investigating of our own?"

"I already have to take over Aqua's usual deliveries." Stevie shook her head. "I know she was friends with one of the maids there. I think her name is Dara something." She shrugged. "Although I don't know how much information I'll be able to squeeze out of the living since they all know me there. I was planning on looking for lurkers and asking *them* what they know."

"Lurkers?" I raised my eyebrows.

"Spirits that don't have much of a purpose," Stevie explained. "They end up lurking around instead of moving on. There are more of those than you would think."

"I could take Aqua's place." I scanned the kitchen. Stevie already had too much on her plate. She would have to multitask, and in my experience that made an employee less efficient. The best thing for me to do would be to step in.

"You? Deliver bread?"

"You said yourself that you hardly recognize me anymore," I went on. "Why not use that to our advantage? Nobody will recognize me, and maybe I can get straight answers from someone."

"I guess that could work." Stevie rubbed the side of her cheek as she considered the suggestion. "I do have a busy day tomorrow, and closing the bakery for a few days sure won't do me any favors."

"Don't you bring in enough money to hire employees or even a general manager?"

"I don't have time to figure that stuff out, Ember. I'm only one person."

"I could take a look—"

"One step at a time," Stevie cut in. "Just because we're talking again doesn't mean we're besties all of a sudden." Her semi-friendly expression was instantly wiped clean. "This is happening because I want Aqua back. I thought I made that clear."

"Your loss," I responded, trying hard to keep my emotions out of it. It would only please Stevie to know that her words stung.

And they did.

"Tomorrow morning. Six o'clock."

"I'll be ready," I said.

"Do you remember how to get to the Crystal Grande?" Her lips twisted with snark as she stood up and resumed her nightly chores.

"I think I can manage it," I answered, seeing the image of the hotel in my mind. It stood overlooking Misty Key, and it had the best beach views from miles around. The hotel was hard *not* to miss.

"Then you'd better get some sleep."

I nodded and headed for the exit located in the back of the kitchen. I had to pass my dad's old office to get to it—an office that had stayed frozen in time. A glance through the open door showed that the pictures on the walls hadn't changed.

"Do you see him much?" I gulped. It was a question I thought about every day but never knew I would have the guts to ask.

"What?" Stevie paused again. Her eyes darted from me to Dad's old office.

"Do you ever see him?" I asked again. "Dad."

Stevie narrowed her eyes as she replied. "All the time."

A knot formed in my stomach and moved all the way up into my lungs, making it hard for me to breathe. The fact that my big sister spoke to the dead was the main reason I'd been avoiding her all these years. It wasn't so much that she was mad at me for leaving when she could've used my help with the bakery. It wasn't her sour feelings toward how my absence had supposedly affected my mother. All of those things could be mended with time.

It was that she could still speak with my father—ask him questions.

"Really?" I forced myself to take a breath, but it was difficult. My lungs felt like two cinder blocks that had been dropped into the middle of the gulf. "Has he mentioned me at all?"

"Nope." Stevie lifted her chin as if she was proud of the fact that any information divulged by my father's ghost was for her ears only.

"Oh." Whether or not she was telling the truth, it still made me as anxious as ever to know that my dad was still around, especially since he knew the thing that had been filling me up with guilt since the day of his death, the real reason I'd made such an effort to start a new life for myself as far away from Misty Key and the Clairs as I could manage.

The moist air hit me as I walked into the humid night, and I dug my fingernails into the palms of my hands. Pressure built behind my eyes as I stared off into the distance at the lights still glowing from various hotel rooms at the Crystal Grande. A part of me was happy to be home, and a part of me felt like I didn't deserve to be back.

I'd spent so much time running only to end up in the same place I'd started.

Somehow, I had to face it.

I had to come clean to someone before the Clairs dished out my punishment and permanently stripped away my gift.

Maybe I deserved it though.

Because *I* was responsible for my father's death.

Chapter 5

Saturday morning came quicker than expected. The sun stayed hidden behind gray storm clouds, allowing the warm fall morning to be overtaken with waves of fog. The cloudy mist floated all through Main Street, and the shopkeepers seemed pleased as they stood outside their establishments with morning mugs of fresh brew. The mist was what tourists expected. After all, it was how Misty Key had gotten its name.

I took the time to check my emails before visiting the bakery. It had been difficult to rub the sleep from my eyes when my alarm had sounded at five o'clock. I struggled to get dressed, feeling as if I were two different people. The more time I spent in my old room, the more I felt like my old self. But the Ember who worked at a successful firm in New York City was who I was now. The Ember from Misty Key had been dead for years.

I focused on Aqua and only Aqua. She was my chance for redemption. If I could figure out what happened to her, my chances at making amends with my family were much higher. I held tight to Stevie's handlebars as I walked her delivery bike up the hill toward the Crystal Grande Hotel. The path had been too steep for me to pedal for much longer, despite my frequent sessions at the gym near my city apartment. The humidity stole all of my energy.

I did my best to catch my breath as I glanced toward the shoreline, where the rolling waves blended into the mist, but I heard the sound of the ocean barreling into the sand. It made me smile. I tugged at the waist of the shorts I'd borrowed from Stevie, who'd insisted that I leave my pencil skirts and muted blazers in my suitcase and wear something more Misty Key appropriate. I'd done just that, although I'd drawn the line at one of her usual tank tops and had opted for a basic polo instead. My caramel locks were back in a tight bun, and I'd chosen to wear my thick-framed glasses—the ones I never wore in public—on the chance that someone recognized me anyway.

The hill rose until a white sandy beach appeared beneath me. The path flattened again, and I hopped on Stevie's bike, one hand on the delivery. As a child, I'd thought of the hotel as a giant seaside castle with ocean perches that housed mermaids and towers that reached the clouds. As an adult, I saw why. A large patio wrapped around the entire side of the building that faced the ocean, and the architecture resembled a historical and spacious plantation home complete with white columns and regal balconies as high as four stories up. The patio was a popular restaurant, and the top-floor balconies flagged the locations of the hotel's most expensive suites.

I cycled around the back of the building where delivery vans made frequent stops and found the back door leading straight into the kitchen and the employee break room. One summer in high school, I took a shift working as a maid for extra cash to go back-to-school shopping. I chuckled to myself, thinking about the things I'd thought were important back then. None of that stuff—boys, bras, my SAT scores—seemed like that big of a deal almost twenty years later.

A delivery man walked past me as I neared the back door.

I hopped off the bicycle and leaned it against a wall. I clutched the satchel of tightly wrapped breads and carefully boxed pastries and went inside. "Excuse me, will someone sign for a bread delivery?"

The employee area of the hotel looked different than I remembered. It was more organized with a wall of lockers, a time clock, and a huge community table between the lounging area and the actual kitchen. I set my delivery basket down on the table and smoothed my polo shirt. I ran a hand over my sweaty forehead and tucked a stray piece of hair behind my ear.

The kitchen was busy.

Employees wearing white aprons with the Crystal Grande logo rushed from counter to counter. Breakfast had begun, and orders for room service were picking up. I took a few steps closer and watched as one of the kitchen staff poached an egg with little effort. It was something I could never do in a million years. Not unless there was a way to make poached eggs using the microwave.

The more I observed, the more I realized I was practically invisible. No one was eager to sign for my order, and no one glanced up and told me to stay away from the room-service cart. The hotel was much busier than I'd expected, considering that the summer was over and the weather was slowly transitioning into the rainy winters I'd once been accustomed to.

"No way. That did *not* happen."

A voice startled me, and I turned to see a group of girls stumbling through the back and toward the employee lockers. I left my delivery of bread on the kitchen table and followed them. Maybe one of them knew my sister. Maybe one of them would loosen her tongue if I approached the subject the right way.

It was worth a try.

"Did you see that bikini she wore yesterday?" one girl asked. "It's like she *wants* to be gossiped about."

"Well, duh," another chimed in. "She doesn't care what kind of attention she gets as long as she's gettin' it."

"Ladies," a voice boomed in their direction. A man in a light blue button-down and matching tie stood in the doorframe. His face was cleanly shaven and his midnight hair matched a mysterious set of eyes. He was slender but still taller than me, and one of his eyebrows rose higher than the other when he grinned. "I hope we're not discussing that latest issue of the *Misty Messenger* featuring a scandalous article on the Carmichael twins."

"Sorry, Magnus," one of the girls replied. "I mean, Mr. Brown." She giggled as she looked at her friend.

"Keep those conversations out of my hotel," Magnus Brown clarified. "And aren't you ladies running a little late?"

"Yes, Mr. Brown. Sorry, Mr. Brown." The girls shoved their purses in their lockers.

Magnus smiled, pleased with their efforts to get to work as soon as possible. His eyes fell to each of them as they silenced their cell phones and prepared for the day. And then his eyes fell to me. He narrowed his gaze when he noticed the absence of a name tag on my shirt.

"Oh, you must be the new girl," he stated, waving a hand. "I wasn't expecting you for another week, but no matter. Come with me. I've got your uniform and name tag in my office."

"Actually—"

"You'll work with Dara today," he added. "She trains all the newbies."

The name *Dara* sank in. I'd heard it before. According to Stevie, Dara was a friend of Aqua's and could possibly shed some light on her whereabouts. I gulped, feeling strange about lying. But all I needed was a few hours of conversation.

I followed Magnus to his office and took a maid's uniform.

"Thanks," I replied, adjusting the rim of my glasses. They must have made me look a little younger.

"Of course, Katie," he continued. "I'm the general manager, so if you have any problems you talk to me." His expression darkened slightly. "We have one *very* important rule around here. If you break it, I'll fire you on the spot."

"Okay," I agreed. Though I tried, I couldn't guess what he was about to say.

"Never, and I mean *never*, talk to Mrs. Carmichael or the Carmichael twins," he stated. "Agreed?"

"Yes, sir."

"Call me Mr. Brown," he responded. "Perhaps Magnus, if you end up staying on."

"Okay, Mr. Brown."

Magnus grinned, but this time his gaze wandered from the point of my knees to the length of my neck. It sent a slight shiver up my spine, and I made a mental note to familiarize myself with the hotel's rules and regulations surrounding their sexual harassment policies. My gut told me there might have been previous incidents documented somewhere.

I spent the next thirty minutes changing into my uniform and looking for Dara on the third floor. My bread delivery had disappeared by the time I'd left Magnus's office and rushed back to the employee lockers. I noticed a pastry or two on a room-service cart as I left the kitchen.

"Are you Katie?" another maid asked when she saw me wandering the halls of the third-floor suites.

I looked down at my name tag to remind myself who I was supposed to be for the day.

"Yes," I answered. "Are you Dara?"

"No, my name is Luann," the women replied. "Dara isn't here yet so you'll be helping me out instead. Welcome to Misty Key. Where did you say you were from? You're a little late in the season for beach bummin'." Luann looked and sounded like a typical Misty Key resident. She had tan lines on her cheeks and red marks on her chest from lying out in the sun too long. Her hair was a light blond, and her southern accent was heavy. She was also very chatty.

"Um, a friend told me about this place," I lied. "Hey, maybe you know her? Her name is Aqua Greene?"

"Oh, Aqua." Luann nodded. "Everybody knows Aqua. Come to think of it, I haven't seen her in a while."

"Do you remember the last time you *did* see her?"

"Well," Luann shrugged as she pushed her cart full of fresh linens and cleaning supplies to our first room at end of the hallway. She knocked on the door before opening it with her keycard. "It must have been a week or two ago."

"And did she seem normal to you?" I asked.

"Well, yeah." Luann wrinkled her nose. "What kind of question is that?" Luann checked the suite before pulling out a checklist. "Okay, girl, the first thing to remember is to turn on all the lights and open the drapes. We need to make sure we can see everything that needs cleaning."

"Okay," I said, following her instructions.

The darkened suite looked even more magical with open windows and lots of natural light. The balcony had a small sitting area and a gorgeous view of the misty beach. The main living space was filled with antique furniture and a minibar. Luann went straight to the kitchenette and checked all the cupboards.

"I like to check for dirty dishes first," Luann said.

I helped her move through each item on her checklist, all the while attempting to bring up Aqua a second time. In my experience, persistence eventually yielded some results.

"So, how long have you been working here?" I asked her as we stripped the king-sized mattress of all of its bedding.

"Oh, I was here back when Mr. Carmichael was still alive," she responded. "A lot of maids have come and gone since then, let me tell you. The hotel has changed so much these past couple of years."

"How do you mean?"

"For one thing, Mrs. Carmichael redesigned the front lobby, and she hired Magnus to do everything for her. I sometimes wonder why she even bothers keeping the hotel, but I guess it's the twins' inheritance so why sell. Have you seen the Carmichael twins yet? They're famous, you know."

"That's what I hear," I commented. My only interaction with Jewel and Jonathon Carmichael consisted of delivering their birthday cake to the hotel one year. They were younger than me—closer to Aqua's age. The Carmichaels were regulars in the local news as well as national news every once in a while. It seemed as if they were always finding new ways to spend the family money. Sometimes tourists camped out near the hotel just to catch a glimpse. Paparazzi were never far from the hotel's private stretch of beach during the summer season. But for locals, and me, the Carmichael twins were just residents of Misty Key who also happened to be wealthy.

"I'm assigned to Jonathon's room on weekends," she proudly stated, biting the corner of her lip. "I had to sign a thing with Magnus before I was allowed in. He's never in his room when I knock, but once I heard his ma shouting something about his gambling debts from the lounge while I was making the bed. Jonathon stormed off before I got to the vacuuming."

"How many maids are assigned to the Carmichaels' rooms?" I pushed my glasses up the bridge of my nose as I searched for the next thing on the checklist.

"Let's see." Luann paused, staring out the window at a break in the clouds. Rays of sunshine began poking through and blue sky loomed in the distance. "There's me, Dara, and..." She sighed, quickly returning to her duties. "So many questions, Katie. Don't worry. If you show up on time and don't piss off any guests, you'll have your turn cleaning a Carmichael suite eventually."

"One can only dream," I muttered.

"You're funny," she exclaimed, letting out a loud chuckle. "Dara is going to like you. She's so serious all the time."

"I think Dara also knows Aqua," I added as we moved on to cleaning the bathroom. So far, scrubbing toilets was my least favorite part of undercover work.

"Oh yeah, I think she does. That's a small town for you." Luann smiled as she wiped down the sink and bathroom mirror. "Geez, is it time for lunch yet? My stomach is rumbling already. Maybe I can snag a swig of sweet tea after we finish this section."

I helped Luann with the rest of her duties. Once everything on our list had been cleaned, we turned off all of the lights and left the room in perfect condition for the next set of guests. I followed Luann to the next room, already dreading my full day of monotony that seemed to be getting me nowhere.

"Remind me to wear more comfortable shoes next time I do something like this," I murmured.

"Hilarious." Luann chuckled as she knocked loudly and opened the door to the next darkened suite. "I swear, the curtains are always closed. Uh, there's a stunning view outside, y'all." Luann shrugged as she pushed the cart of supplies inside.

I did as Luann instructed and turned all of the lights on, but as I approached the windows overlooking the ocean, I realized my path was blocked. Immediately, Luann's breathing rang through the room in short bursts. Most of the muscles in my body tightened as adrenaline pumped through my veins. I wasted no time whipping aside the curtains and letting daylight reveal a scene that made all the warmth drain from my body.

Luann screamed, backing toward the door and knocking over the cart full of linens and cleaning supplies.

"Oh, no," I whispered, looking down at the lifeless body of a young woman wearing a uniform much like mine.

"Dara!" Luann screamed. She covered her face as tears burst from her eyes and dripped down her cheeks.

My eyes darted from Dara's body on the floor to the suite number. The numbers jumped out at me as if trying to warn me of something. My heart pounded as I glanced at the time. *No.* I ran to the mess of supplies near the doorway and grabbed Luann's clipboard. My eyes fell to another number on the empty form she'd previously prepared. *No. No. No.*

Sevens. Too many sevens.

I might have been out of practice, but experience told me one thing about the primary number that continued popping up all over the crime scene.

It was the mark of a witch.

Chapter 6

"I can't breathe."

Luann was on the verge of hyperventilating as I wrapped my arm around her and urged her to drink more water. The police scoured the hotel, and most of the staff were loitering around the large community table in the kitchen.

A man with a dark expression and ebony skin to match paced the room giving orders to various officers in uniform. The man wore a light-colored suit, and his ice blue eyes looked like a glacier in the dead of winter. He approached Luann with a notepad before I had the chance to hide my name tag. Luckily, I didn't know the man, and he didn't know me.

"Luann Watts?" the man inquired. "My name is Detective Winter. When you're ready, I need to ask you some questions about your deceased co-worker."

"What happened to her?" Luann blurted out. "Have you figured out what happened?"

"I assure you that we are taking this matter very seriously," the detective answered. "We are taking time to gather all of the facts before we release a statement to the public."

"Was it a heart attack?" Luann squeezed her hands together. "I didn't see any blood. It had to be a heart attack or something. Oh, why did she have to be alone? Maybe if someone had been with her, she would be alive."

"It's okay, Ms. Watts. We will know for sure after the autopsy." The detective looked at me. "And what's your name?"

"Katie," I said, a little unsure of myself. I pointed to my name tag to emphasize my point. "I'm new."

"Yes, I see that." His face remained expressionless, which I found impressive considering the level of chaos going on around him. "I'll need to speak with you as well."

"Sure." I took a deep breath and forced a smile.

I had to avoid Detective Winter at all costs.

Luckily, he hadn't recognized my voice from our one, very brief, phone call about Aqua's disappearance.

"Excuse me, ladies." The detective looked up when Mrs. Carmichael entered the kitchen. She was wearing a lemon-colored fitted dress and a navy statement necklace that glittered. Her high heels clicked on the tile as she walked toward the detective. The farther she strutted into the room, the more silent the room became.

"Oh my, I haven't seen that woman in months," Luann managed to mutter as she sniffled and dabbed at her cheeks with a tissue.

Mrs. Carmichael, hardly looking at or addressing any of her employees, turned to leave. Detective Winter followed her. The kitchen and adjacent break room area came alive with a wave of chatter once the door had been closed. My mind jumped back to Dara and the signs I'd seen around her body.

A witch resided in Misty Key, and I had to figure out who she was.

"Luann," I said quietly. "You have to help me. There's something I didn't tell you earlier."

"What is it?" She raised her eyebrows.

"Remember my friend Aqua?" I paused, letting Luann come up to speed. "She's missing, and I'm trying to figure out what happened to her."

"You mean like she's out of town?" Luann's eyes widened.

This might have been too much for her to take all at once, but I had no time.

"No, I mean she disappeared without a word and no one has seen her in a week," I stated.

"First Aqua and now Dara?" Luann gasped. "What is going on around here?" The tears returned, and Luann grabbed a new tissue to blow her nose. She sniffled before attempting to pull herself back together.

"Listen to me, Luann," I whispered, glancing over my shoulder at the exit. "The last thing Aqua did before she went missing was make her usual weekly bread delivery. Do you remember *anything* about the last time you saw her? Did she mention anything or anyone?"

Luann sniffled again. "I can't remember exactly, but you could talk to Thad."

"Thad?"

"Mr. Stone's new assistant," Luann responded. "Aqua never left the hotel without saying hello to Thad. Apparently, they hooked up in the boathouse this summer. Just a rumor I heard once. I never had the guts to ask Aqua if it was true."

"Mr. Stone," I repeated carefully. "You don't mean old man Louie, do you?"

"Yeah, Louie Stone. He manages the grounds. I've never spoken a word to him myself, but Mrs. Carmichael seems to like him."

"Great," I muttered. "Where can I find Thad?"

"Oh, uh," Luann scanned the room, wiping another tear that trickled down her face. "He's right there." She pointed to a man, and I wrinkled my nose at the sight of him.

He wasn't Aqua's type at all.

He looked much older than her, and he was free of any tattoos or piercings. Much like my sister

Stevie, Aqua liked to indulge her inner artist. Her carefree attitude had attracted a multitude of personalities. All except for the down-to-earth, sensible ones that you invite home to dinner.

I adjusted my glasses, still not used to wearing them out in public, and patted Luann on the shoulder. Luann nodded back and took a quick sip of her water. The moment I stood up, another maid took my place at her side.

The kitchen was bustling, but no one was working. A couple of line cooks stood near the stove whispering as waiters and waitresses crowded the side entrance to the patio restaurant. In the midst of it all was Thad. I studied him first before approaching him, mostly because I didn't want to run into his boss, Louie Stone. Louie would've recognized me instantly, despite the fact that he hadn't seen me since I was a little girl.

Thad crossed his arms. His dark hair stood out against the beige kitchen backdrop, and he wasn't saying much as he observed the turmoil going on around him. He wore a navy polo bearing the hotel's logo, and his face was cleanly shaven. He definitely wasn't just another college student looking for a seasonal gig. Thad had a specific purpose for being at the Crystal Grande, and maybe I would figure out what it was.

I took a deep breath and looked down at my name tag.

"Hi," I said to Thad as I walked toward him. "I'm Katie."

"Thad," he replied, eyeing my uniform.

"Can you believe all this?" I said, trying to make conversation. I could talk about budgets and strategic marketing all day, but I wasn't great at small talk beyond that. Numbers and facts spoke to me the most.

"Crazy," Thad replied, hardly looking at me.

"Well, did you know Dara?"

"A little," he answered. "I mostly just saw her in passing."

"And do you think she died of a heart attack?"

"Who knows?" Thad shrugged.

The lines on his face gave away his age—mid-thirties at least. His forearms were bulky, and my guess was that he did all of Louie's heavy lifting. But something about him still seemed off. When Thad finally made eye contact, I realized what it was.

He wasn't from Misty Key.

In fact, no part of him was the least bit southern. A number of things gave it away.

So why was he doing manual labor in a little tourist town in southern Alabama?

And had he really been sleeping with my little sister?

"First Aqua, and now Dara," I stated, copying what Luann had said earlier. He blinked when my sister's name escaped my lips. "Did you know Aqua too?"

Thad's eyes narrowed. "How do you know Aqua?"

"She's a friend of mine," I admitted. "And the rumor around here is that she was a friend of yours too."

"*Was?*"

"Haven't you heard?" I continued, finding it frustrating trying to get a reaction from him that extended beyond blinking. "She's missing. The police think she ran away, but I think she was kidnapped."

"Where did you say you're from again?" Thad lifted his chin and studied me suspiciously.

"I didn't." I took a deep breath. "But at least I'm from the south."

"Are you accusing me of something?" Finally, Thad raised his voice.

"You're wearing hiking boots," I pointed out. "It might be autumn everywhere else, but Misty Key stays hot and humid most of the year."

"Maybe I like the way they look," he said. "Or maybe they were a gift. There are lots of explanations for my choice of footwear."

"Whatever the reason, you know Aqua. When was the last time you saw her?"

"I don't have to answer that," Thad replied.

"Not answering implies you're hiding something." I nodded because the statement was a fact I'd validated one too many times. I usually had reason to worry when my latest assistant didn't give me a straight answer. Stacie and the copier incident, for example.

"You didn't tell me where *you* are from, so are you hiding something yourself? Is your name even Katie?"

I cleared my throat, standing up straighter. His accusation wasn't one I'd expected, even though it was a shot in the dark. I shook my head, not knowing how to respond. Thad was acting defensive, which told me that his mind held some crucial details that might help me find my sister.

"Now, son, that's no way to talk to a woman," a voice said from behind Thad.

I clasped my hands together as an older man took his time inching his way into our conversation. The wrinkles on his face and the way he tied his long, gray hair back in a ponytail hadn't changed. His skin was still tan and leathery from decades spent out in the sun, and his hands were scabbed and weathered from years of hard labor. I stared into the face of Louie Stone, unable to avoid it. His beady eyes reminded me of what he really was when the sun went down—a wild animal.

"Sorry, Louie," Thad responded.

"Welcome home, Miss ... *Katie*." Louie glanced down at my name tag and shot me a look of disapproval.

He knew who I was—Ember Greene, unlicensed psychic.

My looks might have changed, but my scent hadn't. Being a chief among the shifters, Louie Stone knew my smell like he knew his own mother. There was no fooling him.

"Thanks," I forced myself to say.

"Wait, you *are* from around here?" Thad questioned me.

My gaze darted to Louie, who just looked at me with a disgruntled expression.

"Yes," I admitted. I fixed my stare on Louie. "And I have to say that something strange is going on around here. It's almost *bewitching*, isn't it?"

The door to the kitchen swung open, and Detective Winter returned with another group of police officers. He announced to the crowd that he would be conducting interviews during work hours over the next couple of days, due to the number of employees the Crystal Grande had on staff. I gulped, knowing that this was my cue to leave. I had to delay my questioning as long as I could. The second Detective Winter did some fact-checking, he would know I was a fraud. And seeing as there was a dead body on a stretcher outside, I couldn't let myself become his number one suspect.

I wasn't responsible.
A local witch was the killer.

Chapter 7

Yogi waited on my bed as I checked my emails. My time spent at the hotel had taken longer than I'd planned and I missed Mr. Cohen's last-minute meeting. I rolled my eyes as I scanned the meeting minutes and saw that one of my co-workers had filled the group in on one of *my* accomplishments. I knew he'd taken credit for it too. He was an Aries. His star sign lived to compete, and he also wanted that director position.

"I should have seen that one coming, Yogi." I shook my head.

But now wasn't the time to dwell on it.

After changing my clothes and putting in contact lenses, I walked to the Lunar Bakery. Yogi followed me, wagging his tail. I was happy to see a long line at the register and Stevie rushing around behind the counter filling orders. The smell was just what I needed to push me out of my mood. The scent of baking bread and the sight of perfectly iced cakes brought back pleasant childhood memories—ones that I hadn't allowed myself to think back on in a while.

"Just a minute, sir." Stevie held up a hand, cutting off one of her customers mid-order. She pulled off her apron and waved at me to follow her to a table in the back of the café where Orion was reading one of his comics and eating a vanilla cupcake.

"Um, are you sure your customers won't get mad?" I asked as the line of people watched her looking confused.

"Oh, they've waited this long. What's one minute longer?"

"That's horrible customer service," I commented, almost embarrassed by the resentful looks we were receiving.

"Do you have news for me or not?"

Yogi sat at my feet and looked up at me as if encouraging me to keep my cool.

"I got a job at the hotel," I responded. "Well, *Katie* got a job as a maid."

"Who's Katie?" Stevie raised her eyebrows.

"That doesn't matter," I said. "What matters is that I'm almost certain that Aqua's disappearance is something *magical*."

"And how do you know that?" Stevie crossed her arms, showing off her sleeve of tattoos.

"It's probably the dead body," Orion chimed in, still staring at his comic. "I got an alert on my phone."

"You mean *my* phone, son." Stevie reached across the table and pocketed the device. "And I heard the sirens."

"I saw the body," I whispered.

Orion dropped his comic book and gave me his full attention.

"Who was it?" Stevie's eyes widened. This was the most interested she'd been in what I had to say in years.

"A maid named Dara," I answered, taking a deep breath. "I read the numbers too."

"Dara, as in Aqua's friend Dara?" Stevie asked.

"Tell me, Stevie, are there any witches living in Misty Key?" My eyes darted to the line as a customer at the back rolled his eyes and stormed out of the bake shop.

"No." Stevie shook her head. "There's been nothing on the registry since the Grant family moved to Cottonberry when I was in high school." Her nostrils flared. Stevie wasn't on friendly terms with Wisteria, Inc., the official North American witch and warlock organization. "Any spellcasters in the area would have to be unregistered."

"In which case, we'll have to file a report with the Clairs before doing anything," I said. "That much I do remember." I hung my head. The paperwork alone would take weeks. "The numbers don't lie, Stevie. There's a witch disturbing the peace in Misty Key."

"You could notify Nova, but your license is expired," Stevie pointed out. "Your reading can't officially go on record."

"I saw what I saw," I added, taking a long, calming breath. A thought occurred to me—a loophole. In my experience, there was always a way around the paperwork if it was needed badly enough. Always. "I'll be back. I have some errands I need to run."

"Wait," Stevie called after me. "Where are you going?"

Yogi trotted along behind me.

"You might get reprimanded for breaking the rules, Stevie, but I won't," I informed her. "I have no license. As far as you know, I'm just a concerned resident asking a few questions."

"And if you find answers?" Stevie raised her eyebrows.

"Then I'll give you exactly what you need to get the Clairs' approval." I nodded confidently, and part of me was confident. I clung to that belief as I rushed back outside into what I'd labeled a southern autumn. The sun peeked through scattered clouds, and the lack of breeze offered little relief from the humidity.

I had an idea, and it required using my gift. I reminded myself that I was doing it for Aqua. All of this was for my kid sister and her safe return. Yogi stuck to my side the way he used to walk beside my dad. I found it hard to look down at his tan coat with hints of auburn. It reminded me too much of Dad's last years. My inner debate continued. There were memories I'd welcomed upon returning home and memories I'd held back.

Maybe one day I wouldn't have to put myself through the kind of inner torment that ended in a sour stomach and me rejecting my past.

I hurried down Main Street toward a place that was sure to force my mind into an instant time hop. But first, I had to pass the Misty Key Marina, where most of the boats in the area stayed docked, and an old friend was sure to notice me. Yogi barked as we passed the calm shoreline. I stared at the rows and rows of fishing boats and small yachts as a subtle ocean breeze stole some of the heat from my face. I was grateful.

"Yogi, come here, you," a voice said from inside a little hut facing the sea. A sign hanging above it said *Pelican Beach Cruises: See Dolphins on Porpoise!* "Don't tell me you escaped again, boy. Your mama don't like that."

"He's with me," I said, stepping into full view.

The woman in the hut gasped. "Well, I'll be darned."

I hadn't seen Rickiah Pepper in a long time, and it was a relief to see that her first reaction wasn't to tell me off for not calling her since I'd left for New York City.

"Girl, you have a lot of nerve coming to see me without an apology present," Rickiah stated. She pursed her glossy lips and glared at me the way Stevie glared at Orion when he went to bed without brushing his teeth.

"I'll make it up to you," I promised. "Is a check okay?" I paused, hoping Rickiah hadn't lost her refreshing sense of humor.

"Make sure you spell my name right this time." She walked onto the sidewalk and hugged me. Her black curly hair was shiny, and her skin reminded me of a sequined bronze ball gown. It was something I'd been jealous of when we were younger. Rickiah's hair was always perfect, and she never burned when we lay out on the beach. Not to mention, I'd never heard her say anything bad about herself. Her confidence hadn't wavered in the twenty-plus years I'd known her. I'd always admired her for that.

"Ricki with an *i*, not a *y*. I got it."

"I hope you've found some answers since getting here," she commented. "It's out of character for Aqua to leave your mama hangin' like that. I mean, I assume that's why you're here?"

I'd never been able to keep anything from Rickiah. It was as if she were psychic herself. She wasn't, but she'd known all about my family and me since we were kids. Rickiah was my only non-mystical friend who knew everything about my gift.

She knew about the Clairs. She knew that my mom had prophetic dreams and that Stevie could talk to the dead. The only thing she didn't know was my secret about my dad. That, I hadn't told anyone.

"I wish that wasn't the reason, but yes."

"In that case, let me know if I can do anything to help," Rickiah replied, reaching down to scratch behind Yogi's ears.

"Actually, there is something you can do." I took a moment to look out at the ocean. The waves were calm, and boats sat comfortably in their spots as if they were nestled in a comfy bed. I wished my life could be just as serene.

"I'm not privy to Aqua's social life," Rickiah said. "An old fart like me."

"We're the same age," I pointed out.

"We're dinosaurs compared to that twenty-something crowd." She placed a hand on her hip. "But I do know that she had been acting a little off the past month. Not as chatty."

"So you two never got together on the weekends or anything?"

"No. She rode past here on her bicycle a lot. Didn't even stop most of the time. She was a girl on a mission, that's for sure." Rickiah pursed her lips again.

"If she rode by here a lot then I'm headed in the right direction," I replied.

"How do you mean?"

"I was going to see Gator to ask him some questions. If my sister passed by here a lot then she must have been going to see him."

"What for?" Rickiah wrinkled her nose in confusion.

"I'm about to find out. You'll be hearing from me. I mean it this time." I cleared my throat and waved goodbye to Rickiah, whistling at Yogi to follow me. He tore himself away from Rickiah's warm embrace and ran to catch up with me.

"Ember," Rickiah shouted. "Wait!"

I stopped suddenly, forcing Yogi to hit the back of my knees with enough force to make me stumble.

"Yeah?"

"You forgot my check," Rickiah shouted back.

* * *

Past Main Street and the Misty Key Marina stood a small group of shops utilized mostly by locals. There was a quaint grocery store, the Misty Key Bank, a row of medical offices, and the one drugstore in town, which was run by a man the locals called Gator.

I didn't know Gator's real name, and I doubted that many people did, but I'd heard the story of how he'd gotten his nickname hundreds of times. From Gator. The story was never the same, but the gist of it involved a baby getting lost in the swamps and being taken in by a gracious family of alligators. I laughed every time Gator mentioned it as if it were fact.

Gator's great-grandmother had been a psychic, so he knew that not every person roaming the streets of Misty Key was human, but that didn't seem to bother him. Instead, he'd used his knowledge to his advantage by building up a little side business. He was known amongst the magical folks in the area as an errand boy. Anything they needed, somehow he was able to find it.

If there had been an uptick in witchy activity, he would know about it.

I entered the shop, and nothing about it had changed. There was a display of candy at the register where I used to grab a last-minute Moon Pie. The cosmetic aisle was in the same place. I had tons of memories of myself pacing that stretch of flooring trying to decide on lipstick and nail polish shades. I noticed a mop of gray hair at the pharmacy counter. Miss Betty was still there dispensing medications. Cameras sat in every corner and Yogi jogged straight back toward the restrooms where Gator would surely be sitting in his office.

Yogi barked, announcing my arrival.

Gator sat with his feet up on his desk. A replay of a previous night's Alabama football game flashed on the screen. Gator sat up when he saw me, taking a moment to place my familiar features.

"Nice to see you, Gator," I said.

"Wait a minute," he responded, tilting his head. "Nah, it can't be. Ember, is that you?"

"In the flesh."

"I scared you off that night I asked you out, didn't I?" he teased. His cheeks dimpled as he rubbed his facial hair—a distinct pattern running underneath his chin that Gator had referred to as a chin strap. He hadn't changed his look since. He leaned back in his seat, pausing the TV and revealing a round belly that matched his round face.

"What can I say, you're just too much man for me," I joked back.

Yogi nudged the side of my knee.

"So, what can I do for you?"

"I need to see your books," I responded.

"Oh, I know we're old friends, but I can't be giving out folks' information." He stroked the side of his face, his eyes darting to the frozen scene on the TV. "You understand, right?"

"I'm not asking to see names," I said. I paused and took a deep breath, calming my mind. "I just need to see your recent inventory records."

"Why?"

"Please, Gator."

"Am I being audited or something?" Gator said, looking confused. "Where did you say you worked nowadays? Does it start with an *I* and end in *R-S*?"

"No, this has nothing to do with whether you do or don't pay taxes," I responded. "Look, if you won't do it for me then do it for Aqua."

Gator picked up his remote and turned the TV off. He focused on me for a moment, letting our eyes meet. He'd aged a little, but his demeanor was still the same. He'd known me all his life. He knew my family, and he'd known my dad. I knew that Aqua's safety meant something to him. It had to.

"So, she's still missing?" he asked softly.

"Coming up on a week."

"I'm sorry, Ember." He sighed. "I wish I could tell you it'll all be okay, but we live in a crazy world."

"I know she came to see you a few times," I said, my voice unwavering. Although I didn't have much evidence to prove it, I felt it in my gut. "I take it you still do a little business on the side?"

"I have been known to break out my granny's old moonshine recipe now and again," he stated. "I never sold any to Aqua though."

"But you've found things for my family and me in the past," I stated. "Things that are hard to come by."

"Oh, yes." Gator nodded. "*Those* things."

"What did Aqua want?" I asked. My heart raced as I eagerly awaited his answer.

"Come with me."

Gator stood up and led me to the employee break room. Miss Betty entered holding a set of keys in her hand, and Gator froze in his tracks. I smiled and nodded at Miss Betty as she scowled in Gator's direction.

"I'm going on my break," she said rather glumly. "I'll be back when I'm back." She skulked toward the fridge and scanned the contents inside.

"All right," Gator agreed. "And don't touch my pimiento. I just about fired you last week when you threw out that corn pudding I was saving."

Miss Betty rolled her eyes as she grabbed a pink lunch bag.

"You say that every day," she murmured as she left the room.

Gator glanced out into the hall and watched her go. When he was satisfied that we wouldn't be interrupted, he shut the break room door and opened the cupboard under the sink. He fiddled with a loose piece of wood that sat up against the back wall. Gator pulled the wood away and grabbed a black book with various scratches on the cover. He sat at the table and thumbed through the pages, stopping at the last bit of entries.

"It's all right here," he said, showing me the list of transactions. "She came to me wanting a few things for some sort of skin paste she wanted to try?"

"Lemongrass," I read out loud. "Red pepper. Hawthorn berries. Bauhinia flowers?" My eyes widened as I looked at him. "*Deer tongue.*"

"Yeah, I have to admit that one was a little weird." He shrugged.

"These are standard potion ingredients," I exclaimed, smacking him over the head. "Why didn't you say something?" My heart pounded and a rush of anxiety came over me. If Gator had opened his mouth and reported something to someone, Aqua might have been spared.

"How was I supposed to know that?" he argued. "You know me. I don't like to ask questions."

I grabbed the book and flipped through the pages myself. My heart rate didn't slow as my eyes darted from one ingredient to another. I did my best to index them in my mind, naturally assigning numbers to every item until I found a pattern.

"You sell a lot of lavender," I commented. "You should grow it on your own. You'd make more money that way."

"I'll make a note of that." Gator twisted his lips as he tried to make himself comfortable in his seat.

I pulled a pen from my purse and ripped a blank sheet of paper from Gator's black book of transactions. He winced at the sound of tearing paper, but I focused on what I was good at. I made a list of dates and ingredients going back a few months. Yogi paced back and forth in front of the door as I copied as much information as I could.

Numbers jumped out at me left and right. My gift was among the most useful of my kind when it worked. My problem was that it seemed to come and go, regardless of whether I needed it or not. Though I'd tried many times, I had little control over it. Sometimes I just got lucky. The Clairs, and even Lady Deja herself, had suggested that I practice regular meditation years ago before Dad passed away.

I'd done what they'd suggested but it hadn't helped.

When I was finished copying Gator's ledger, I wrote down two numbers that I couldn't get out of my head and handed them to him. Gator stared at the numbers with a confused look on his face. I closed his book and slid it across the table.

"What's this?" He held the piece of paper up.

"It's your fortune," I replied with a slight chuckle. I hadn't done a reading for anyone since leaving Misty Key, but the numbers were there, and I figured I owed Gator something in return.

"What sort of fortune is this?" he asked.

"I don't know." I shrugged. "But numbers are connected to everything in the universe somehow.

Do any of those numbers look familiar? Birthdays? Ages? Important dates?"

Gator shook his head. "I believe you've lost your touch."

"I might be wrong sometimes, but the numbers aren't," I disagreed. "Maybe it has to do with the store. Maybe they're product numbers."

Gator raised his eyebrows as he pocketed the information, grabbed his black book, and nestled it safely back in its hiding place. I followed him back to his office, where he immediately switched on the TV as if our little meeting had never happened. Yogi wagged his tail, waiting patiently in the doorway. I was glad I had him to keep me on track.

"Best of luck to you," he said lowly. "I hope you find your sister."

"Me too."

"And shred that information when you're done with it," Gator added, pointing a finger in my direction. "If the tax man comes knocking on my door, you'll be hearing from me, and it won't be pretty."

"I haven't ratted you out so far." I was smiling as I followed Yogi back outside into the warm humidity.

I placed my hands in my pockets as I followed Yogi back toward Main Street. My hand clutched the folded piece of paper. I was confident that if I studied it, I would figure out what Aqua was doing making so many purchases over the last month—and buying common potion supplies to boot. But it all fit together somehow.

Potions.

Witches.

Dead bodies.

Thad?

Yogi turned to look at me when I stopped, seeing a familiar face in the distance. Thad was standing outside the grocery store and scanning the front windows as he walked toward me. I frowned, wondering what he was doing at this end of town when there was a murder investigation being conducted at the hotel. He continued walking toward Gator's drugstore, and I carefully inched farther away from the entrance.

Eventually, his wandering gaze fell to Yogi.

And then to me.

"Thad," I said in as friendly of a tone as I could muster. "What are you doing here? Aren't you supposed to be working?"

"Aren't you?" he said. He'd changed out of his uniform—jeans, a plain T-shirt, and the same out-of-season hiking boots. *Definitely not a southerner.*

"They let me go early," I lied.

"Well then, they let me go early too," he copied me. "See you tomorrow."

I nodded and continued walking, pretending that I had other things on my mind. When I'd walked farther away, I casually glanced over my shoulder and watched as Thad walked into Gator's drugstore. Yogi barked as if he could read my thoughts.

"I agree," I told him as we approached the Misty Key Marina once more. "Very suspicious."

Chapter 8

I jerked awake at the sound of my alarm. I was face down at the kitchen table with papers heaped at my fingertips. My phone buzzed, and I scrambled to silence it while attempting to shield my eyes from the rays of sunshine peeking through the skylights. I rubbed my eyes, smearing a bit of yesterday's mascara. I must have looked like a raccoon. A tired raccoon.

Crunch.

I rubbed my temples as I let my brain catch up with the present.

Crunch. Crunch.

Orion sat in his usual spot at the kitchen table chomping on his cereal and watching me like a morning cartoon. I sighed and tried to make myself look presentable by pinching my pale cheeks, running my fingers through a knot of tousled hair, and forcing a smile. My efforts made Orion giggle. Yogi, who had been sleeping at my feet, rose from his slumber.

"Do they have beds in New York City?" Orion took another bite of his chocolaty Crunch-O's.

"Yes, and I own one of them," I responded, eyeing the empty coffeemaker on the counter. "You sound just like your mom sometimes."

"Mom sleeps in on Sunday mornings, and Granny goes to brunch with the society ladies. Kids aren't allowed."

"For good reason," I added. I gathered up my papers and got up in search of caffeine.

The back door swung open, and Yogi rushed to greet Stevie and my mother. They were deep in conversation. I squinted for a minute and adjusted my jaw.

"Morning, Ember," Stevie said. "You're looking rough." She nudged my shoulder as she opened a nearby cupboard and produced the coffee I'd been looking for. "By the way, one of your cheeks is red."

I took a deep breath and rubbed both cheeks. One of them did feel sore. It must be the side of my face I'd slept on. I played with my jaw again.

"You two are up early," I commented.

"Well, your sister has been trying to get a read on that dead girl," my mother explained. She barely flinched at the mention of the horrible incident that had occurred the previous day at the Crystal Grande Hotel. "We've been all over town. And that salmon-colored wallpaper Mrs. Carmichael put in the Crystal Grande lobby is so refreshing. I think I might steal that shade for the front door. Speaking of which, I could use a sweet tea."

"Are you allowed to look for her spirit like that without permission?" I asked, not the least bit surprised.

"It wasn't an official reading," Stevie replied. "I'm just a concerned resident asking a few questions." She grinned and filled a mug with tap water. She took a sip as she leaned against the counter and watched the coffeemaker in action.

"I hope you have answers," I responded. "What did Dara say? Was she murdered? Was it a witch?"

"If it were that easy, there would be a lot less psychos in the world," she answered. "I tried to make contact with Dara's spirit, but I got nothing."

I rubbed my forehead.

"We'll keep trying," my mom said firmly. Her voice was slightly shaky as it always seemed to be when we talked about Aqua. "We have a friend in the coroner's office. One of these days, Dara will be willing to talk."

"Unless someone has cast a binding spell." Stevie bit the inside of her cheek, still watching the coffee drip into the pot. "If that's the case, then her spirit will never be able to talk to me."

"Witches," I muttered. "I'm telling you, someone in Misty Key is a liar and a killer."

"I did get a witchy vibe at the hotel," Stevie agreed. "I think it was a spell that killed her. The question is why Dara? It's the off-season for sirens. She wasn't in anyone's way."

"Wait." My eyes grew wide. "Dara was magical?"

"If you count singing to the tide as a magical talent. Did I forget to mention that?" Stevie narrowed her eyes as she observed my expression.

"Now, gals, this isn't a contest," Mom said. "Ember, you must have come up with some information. What did you find?"

"Aqua bought supplies from Gator, and her purchases coincide with the bakery's delivery schedule," I stated as I held up my papers. "So, basically every time she made a delivery to the hotel, she also stopped at Gator's for something." I held up a finger. "Except for the very end of the month last month. The purchases went from a lot to none, and they started back up again at the beginning of *this* month."

"Who do you think she was buying for?" Stevie asked.

"Someone at the hotel," I answered. "It all adds up. She drops off the bread and collects orders. Has she made any other out-of-the-ordinary purchases lately?"

"No." My mother shook her head and rubbed the moonstone that hung around her neck. "No new clothes. No shopping sprees. Her schedule was pretty normal."

"I didn't notice anything either," Stevie added.

"If she wasn't doing it for extra cash, then why bother?" I scratched the side of my head. "And why didn't she say anything?"

"Maybe she was being blackmailed?" Orion proceeded to pour a second bowl of cereal. "It happens all the time in my comics. It's how good guys turn into bad guys. They're forced to do it."

"Now there's something I hadn't thought of." My mom dropped into the nearest chair.

Stevie prepared an extra mug and watched the coffeemaker a few minutes longer. As soon as the fresh brew was done, she poured some for Mom and herself. I waited until she was finished gathering creamer and poured a mug for myself.

"Can I have some?" Orion asked.

"Are you really asking me that?" Stevie answered. Orion shook his head.

"I just don't understand," my mother breathed. "Why would anyone want to harm my little Aqua?"

"Witches are vengeful," Stevie scoffed. "I've never met one I liked."

"*Honey*," Mom scolded her. "As keepers of the peace, we don't pass judgment."

"Yada yada." Stevie shook her head. "I just never thought this would turn into a witch hunt."

I took a sip of my coffee without adding anything to it. The taste wasn't pleasant without my usual cream and sugar, but I needed the bitter kick to keep me going. I glanced at the time. I was late for work. Or rather, *Katie* was late for work. If I was going to find out the identity of the secret witch at the Crystal Grande Hotel, then I had to keep roaming the halls and trying to get more readings.

If the numbers would cooperate.

I took another gulp, grabbed my papers, and headed for the door.

"Where are you going?" Stevie called after me. "The bakery is closed today. We have more people to question."

"You go ahead," I replied. "I'm late for work."

"I knew it." Stevie rolled her eyes. "One lead, and she's out. I told you, Ma. I told you she wouldn't stay."

"I'm late for work at the Crystal Grande," I clarified. "We have a better chance of identifying the rogue spellcaster if one of us is there most of the time. The witch has got to make a mistake sooner or later. The police are all over that place."

"Oh." Stevie stared down into her mug. "Good luck then."

"Yeah." I nodded. "I'll need it."

I grabbed my uniform and yelled goodbye to Yogi as I ran outside. Running all the way there was my fastest option, considering the weekend traffic on Main Street. It wasn't that there were tons of cars. The streets were just narrow, and a few extra vehicles blocked up the roundabout in front of Town Square.

I huffed as I ran up the hill with a gorgeous view of the sea to keep me company. Tomorrow was Monday, and unless Aqua appeared by nightfall, my chances of catching my flight back to NYC were slim. It made my stomach churn to think of the look on Mr. Cohen's face when he found my office empty tomorrow morning. But I'd made a promise to Aqua, and now to Stevie too.

I didn't know what to do.

I'd worked so hard to climb the ladder at Fillmore Media, but I couldn't just leave my family when they needed me the most, despite Stevie's snide comments. I had to make some decisions, and they were decisions I didn't want to make. My fears about returning to Misty Key were slowly coming true. One fear being that I might never return to my life in New York.

* * *

"It's wrong. It's all wrong. Take it down and start over." Mrs. Carmichael folded her arms. A near-permanent scowl hung on her face as she watched a couple of her employees hang strands of lights in the lobby. She was wearing a plum-colored sundress and large, dangly earrings with orange stones in the center.

I hurried toward the kitchen and the employee break room, thinking that I would eventually run into the police, but I had yet to see an officer or be asked any questions.

After only an hour, Magnus Brown had already sent me on various errands because he was short-staffed. I sat down at the large table to catch my breath.

"Katie," a voice whispered. "Hello, Katie?"

It took me a minute to remember that *I* was Katie.

I turned around to find Luann watching me suspiciously.

"Oh, Luann," I responded. "I thought you had a few days off."

"That was the plan," she answered. "Until Mr. Brown called me this morning saying that we're short-staffed. I could always use the extra cash, especially now that my mama is on medication for her high blood pressure. She watches too many daytime soaps. I think they stress her out."

"Right." I nodded as I adjusted the rims of my glasses—*Katie's* glasses. "It's quiet around here. I mean, it's quiet without the police around."

"The rumor is that Dara died of heart complications if you can believe that," Luann answered. "I guess the police are backing off."

"How tragic. She was young, right? Though I suppose that's better than all of us being suspects." I didn't believe the reasoning for a minute, but I did feel sympathy for Dara.

"You know, if you ask me, I think Mrs. Carmichael had a hand in that. I heard she wasn't too happy with the way they paraded around the hotel. Several guests complained."

"Oh." I raised my eyebrows and pretended to be surprised. But inside, I let out a sigh of relief.

"Mr. Brown told me to pair up with you today." A faint smile crossed Luann's face. "We've been assigned to the Carmichaels' floor." Her eyes widened, and by the look on her face, I would never have guessed that a friend of hers had just died. "Isn't that exciting?"

"Really? Me?" I instinctively glanced over my shoulder, wondering if Luann had been referring to someone else.

"Yes, you." Luann giggled as she grabbed my arm. "Now, come on. You have some forms to sign before I can take you up to clean their suites."

Luann happily ushered me into Magnus's office where a packet of legal work was waiting for me. Magnus explained that signing the documents meant that I wasn't allowed to say anything about what I heard or saw upon entering any of the Carmichaels' suites. Punishment involved me, or rather Katie, being fired and possibly sued. I quickly realized as I scribbled a fake, illegible signature on each page that Magnus had given Luann this particular assignment on purpose because he knew it would cheer her up.

And he'd been right.

The second my paperwork was sorted, Luann grabbed me by the hand and led me through the lobby, where Mrs. Carmichael was still barking orders to several staff members. She rolled her eyes, stopping to smile at passing guests, but then immediately resumed her look of utter disappointment. Luann and I tiptoed past her on our way upstairs.

"She's been in a rotten mood all morning," Luann muttered when we were out of earshot. "I heard she's hosting some charity thingy tonight and it's all very last minute. Apparently, she doesn't even have a dress for the occasion."

"So, Mrs. Carmichael actually has to work today."

"Just like the rest of us common folk," Luann teased. "And she ain't too happy about it." She tucked a strand of blond hair behind her ear.

The way to the Carmichael suites wasn't well known. It consisted of taking a private elevator that was situated in a quiet part of the main floor. It was hidden behind a heavy door that blended in with the floral wallpaper. The hairs on the back of my head stood straight up as we waited to step into the elevator. I glanced up and happened to look directly at a security camera looming overhead.

When the elevator finally arrived, one of the twins stepped out. Jewel barely batted an eyelash, taking no notice of us as she zipped up her purse and prepared to strut into the lobby where her mother would surely chastise her for her choice of clothing.

Or, rather, her lack thereof.

Jewel Carmichael, one of the famous Carmichael twins, was younger than me, in her early twenties. She wore a sheer slip that revealed a red bikini underneath that was so tiny she might as well have been wearing nothing. She glossed her lips, stepping onto the shiny lobby floor with a pair of dark sunglasses and high heels that matched her swimwear. It didn't seem sunny enough to soak up the rays, but my guess was that she wanted to show off the results of her latest cosmetic enhancement.

Luann looked down as she stepped aside and I found it strange to watch. It was as if Luann regarded Jewel as royalty, and we were the Carmichaels' faithful servants. I took a deep breath, unhappy with the attitude Luann had adopted toward a pair of spoiled children who had no idea what it was like to work for a living.

"Let's go." I nudged her shoulder and entered the elevator as soon as it was vacant. Luann entered a code—one that changed daily, I'd learned. We stood in silence until the doors opened again.

I stepped into a long, well-lit hallway with three doors. I assumed that one door led to Mrs. Carmichael's suite, one to Jewel's suite, and finally one to Jonathon's suite. I watched as Luann unlocked a storage closet next to the elevator and pulled out a special cleaning cart. She pushed it toward one of the doors, and her hands shook slightly as she unlocked it.

Jonathon Carmichael's suite looked like the aftermath of a frat party. I wrinkled my nose in disgust at the garbage on the floor, counters, and couch. Judging from the smell, there was at least one splatter of puke somewhere. I walked straight toward the curtains and opened the windows, allowing an ocean breeze to provide my nostrils with some relief.

Jonathon wasn't there. He was most likely at the hotel restaurant having his breakfast and drinking off a nasty hangover. I shook my head, disappointed that a person would treat such a gorgeous room with such disrespect. All of the furniture was southern antiques. A beautiful painting of the ocean hung over a wooden mantelpiece. Even the curtains were heavy and most likely hand-sewn. I rolled my eyes when I noticed the googly-eyed smile on Luann's face. She grabbed a trash bag and started by cleaning up the garbage strewn all over the place.

"This floor was designed by Mr. Carmichael himself," Luann said as she scooped plastic cups into her bag. "He wanted to make sure his family had all the privacy they needed. One of the legacies he left behind was this portion of the hotel. He designed each room himself before he died. Isn't it wonderful?"

"All that's missing is a half-dressed tramp stumbling out of the closet," I muttered.

"Huh?"

"Oh, nothing." I shrugged and continued picking up trash. I cringed when I found a stain on the rug in the sitting area. "Um, what should I do about this?"

Luann glanced at the stain like it was just another dirty dish to load into the dishwasher.

"Oh, we have stuff that can take care of that," Luann responded. "And when we can't get the stains out, we fill out a form and give it to Mr. Brown."

"So, he'll just replace it?" I asked. My eye studied the intricate detail along the rug's edges. I'd seen one like it before at a hotel in New York City. "This rug probably cost thousands of dollars."

"It's no big deal to the Carmichaels," Luann said.

My stomach went sour at the thought of all that wasted family money. The hotel's books must be a nightmare if they spent money replacing things that the Carmichael twins had ruined. Part of me wondered if their absent father was partly to blame for their erratic behavior.

"Oh, shooting stars, that's gross," I gasped as I flipped a couch cushion. A plate of what looked like fried chicken and collard greens had been mashed into the upholstery.

And it had been sitting there all night long.

I plugged my nose. I didn't understand why Luann didn't seem to mind. How was cleaning up after one of Jonathon's crazy parties a privilege? Why didn't his mother make him clean up his own crap for a change? The mixture of smells gathered in my nose and made me feel queasy. I tried not to think of the rotting food, the puddles of vomit, and what was sure to be a disgusting display of who-knew-what when we changed the sheets in the bedroom.

"Are you okay, Katie?"

"Yeah, I just need a minute." I pushed open the door to the balcony and stepped outside to catch my breath.

The view was serene, and I wished that I could have stayed out on the patio all day. Small waves rolled in and out of the shoreline. The sand looked sugary white, and the water was a clear blue when it was touched by the sun. There were gray clouds in the distance, but the warm, humid morning was good enough weather for a few guests to stroll along the coastline. Jewel included.

A commotion of photographers stood near the hotel's entrance, blocked from entering the private beach where Jewel walked carefully in her bikini. I shook my head at the sight of it all. She pretended not to notice the cameras as she held poses and photographers snapped her picture from a distance. It was something I wasn't used to seeing.

I scanned the rest of the beach before going back inside. My eyes darted from guest to guest until they stopped on one person in particular. My body froze. I could hardly take a breath. The air was warm and humid, but my skin turned to ice.

Someone was standing on the beach and looking straight up at me.

He was unmistakable and a potential roadblock in Aqua's investigation.

It was Louie Stone, the groundskeeper, and he was glaring at me in the unfriendliest of ways.

Chapter 9

The clan of shifters in Misty Key wasn't happy.

I resumed my cleaning duties thinking of the look on Louie's face. He must have picked up my sent on the wind and had known that I would be standing outside on Jonathon's balcony. He knew my real identity. He knew I wasn't Katie. He also knew that he could report me to the Clairs if I was becoming a nuisance to him or anyone in his clan. Unfortunately, the fact that my Seer license was expired would mean that being reprimanded for meddling would come with harsher consequences.

Before I had time to think about a solution to my new problem, Luann grabbed my wrist and dragged me to the master bathroom. I narrowed my eyes as she gasped and checked her appearance in the mirror. The front door clicked and the sound of footsteps pittered around the sitting area. My heart raced, but Luann's grin grew wider.

"It's Jonathon," she whispered excitedly. "Just act natural."

"No problem."

Luann handed me a sponge and pointed to the sink. I began scrubbing the tiles in the bathroom as she walked carefully back into the living room where she was still picking up trash. I peeked around the corner and observed as Jonathon walked right by her a couple of times as if she didn't exist. His nose was buried in his cell phone, and his hair was a mess. He was shorter than he appeared to be in magazines and not at all as attractive as his sister, Jewel. But he was still rich.

I continued cleaning the bathroom, wondering what it would take to get a simple *hello* out of him. Maybe it took knocking one of us over or tripping into our cleaning cart. Either way, I couldn't help but roll my eyes and think about all the time I was wasting in Jonathon's room when I could have been snooping around the Crystal Grande learning more about Dara. And, by extension, my sister Aqua.

"Ugh."

The sound of Jonathon's voice made me stop what I was doing and peek into the sitting area a second time. Jonathon had just attempted to sit on the couch amongst the grease stains and rotting collard greens—a mess he'd made himself.

"My apologies, sir," Luann replied without hesitation. "I'll take care of those stains right away."

Jonathon raised his thick brows as he opened his mouth. I guessed that he had a fleet of foul replies on his tongue, but he stopped after taking a second to look at Luann. His gaze wandered up and down her uniform, and his look of disgust quickly turned into a leer.

"No apologies necessary," he slyly replied. His hair was darker and thick. His short and stalky stature reminded me of the portrait of Mr. Carmichael that was hanging in the hotel lobby. "You're just doing your job, Miss ..."

"Luann," she excitedly answered. "My name is Luann, Mr. Carmichael."

"Oh please, call me Jonathon."

"Okay." Luann covered her mouth, suppressing a burst of giggling.

Luann's response seemed to please him. Jonathon took a step closer to her and placed a hand on her shoulder. His stubby fingers rubbed the side of her arm and slowly moved down toward her wrist. "I'm very sorry about the loss of your co-worker. You must be devastated."

"Very," Luann replied. "She was a good friend of mine."

"Was she now?" Jonathon's hands interlocked with hers. "I had no idea. You must have a drink with me in her honor."

Jonathon wasted no time letting go of Luann's hand and digging up a couple of clean glasses. His wild party from the night before might have been over, but he had no problem producing a full bottle of alcohol. He poured two glasses of champagne to the rim and handed one to Luann.

"Thanks." Luann blushed, completely smitten with Jonathon's proposal.

"To Dara." He held his glass in the air.

"To Dara," Luann repeated.

They clinked their glasses. Luann drank, and Jonathon took a small sip, keeping his eyes focused on Luann's bun of blond hair. The look on his face reminded me a bit of the look I'd seen Magnus give a few of the maids. It was a look I sometimes saw back at the New York office before new, male employees learned that my position was higher than theirs. I hated that look of superiority. I didn't have to be a mind-reader to know what Jonathon was thinking. His expression and lengthy portfolio of scandalous magazine articles spoke for themselves.

I took a deep breath and cleared my throat as I entered the room. Disappointment flashed in Luann's eyes, but I was doing her a favor. Jonathon wasn't the sort of man who thought about the feelings of others. I forced a smile, letting my intuition lead me down a different path.

"Yes," I said quietly, adjusting my glasses. I grabbed the bottle of champagne and pretended to take a swig. "To Dara."

Jonathon stared at me for a moment before chuckling to himself.

I'd convinced him that I was okay with bending the rules.

"Well then, ladies. Welcome to the after-party," he mischievously declared. "In Dara's honor, of course."

"Of course," I repeated. Maybe acting had been a hidden talent of mine because Jonathon didn't seem wary of my presence.

"Yes." Luann giggled again.

Jonathon held up his glass and chugged the rest of his drink. I immediately refilled it. Luann ran her fingers through her hair and pushed out her chest. I tried to think of an effective way to ask Jonathon about Dara's death as he downed more champagne. He'd obviously known her. Luann hadn't mentioned her name once, but it'd seemed to flow easily from Jonathon's mouth.

"We miss Dara," I added, looking to Luann.

"Yes, we miss her a lot." Luann didn't seem to care that I hadn't even met Dara. She was too fixated on Jonathon, and I knew that all she wanted was for him to sweep her off her feet and whisk her away like a princess. That wasn't going to happen. My gut told me that the only *whisking* Jonathon wanted to do was off to the bedroom.

"She talked about you all the time," I commented.

"Did she?" Jonathon looked intrigued rather than confused. "I take it she told you about our little … *arrangement*."

"Uh—"

"Discreetly." I cut off Luann with a fake giggle. The sound of it made me want to gag.

"Well then, you know I'll be looking for a replacement." Jonathon raised his eyebrows.

"Replacement?" Luann questioned.

Jonathon paused and twisted his mouth in confusion.

"We're interested," I blurted out. I stepped forward and touched his bicep, letting my eyes lock with his. It took everything I had not to clench my jaw and mutter what I really thought of him out loud.

"Okay." Jonathon nodded, looking pleased with himself. I refilled his glass again, and he wasted no time drinking it. "The two of you and me. We'll see who has what it takes."

Jonathon winked at me as he untucked his shirt.

I glanced at Luann, who was still a little confused.

"Excuse us," I responded. "The two of us need a minute."

Jonathon tilted his head suspiciously.

"Uh—"

"I mean we need a minute to prepare," I went on, talking over Luann. "Come on, Luann."

I grabbed her by the hand and led her straight back to the master bathroom, where I closed and locked the door behind us. I rolled my eyes, pacing the tiled floor and trying to collect my thoughts. Dara and Jonathon had known each other. They'd known each other *very* well.

"Katie, what's the matter with you?" Luann whispered.

"Okay." I looked in her direction, pulling myself out of a storm cloud of theories. "Sorry, I've always sucked at foreplay. You'll have to do that part."

"What are you talking about?" Luann scratched the side of her head.

"We're not going to sleep with him, obviously," I stated, wrinkling my nose. "Gross. We just need to work him up a little and get some more information."

"Katie, you're not making any sense."

It finally dawned on me that Luann wasn't up to speed and that her actions had all been genuine. She had a crush on Jonathon, and she wanted to be with him. But her naïveté was clouding her judgment. Had Jonathon played the same games with Dara? Was Dara a willing participant, and what exactly had her arrangement with Jonathon entailed? Maybe it involved *singing to the tide*, as Stevie had described earlier.

"Crap." I sighed, taking off my glasses for a moment and reminding myself that though I may not have looked it, I was at least ten years older than her. "Luann, Jonathon is a sleazebag in search of a new toy."

"Huh?"

"He wants a little maid-on-maid action," I explained, gagging at the thought.

"What?"

"He wants to sleep with you. Me. Both of us. Who knows? This is straight out of one of your mom's soap operas. I can see why they stress her out so much."

"He does?" Luann practically gasped. Her wide-eyed expression reminded me of an innocent doe.

"Not because he likes us, Luann," I continued. "He's just a spoiled little rich boy with no respect for women. And I won't let you end up like Dara."

"I don't understand." Luann's expression lost a bit of its luster as her shoulders sank in remorse at the mention of Dara's name.

"You will eventually." I placed my hands on her shoulders and nodded assuredly. "Let me do the talking."

The two of us walked out into the bedroom. I cleared my head and thought of Dara, but a rush of anxiety clouded my head at the thought of another innocent maid falling prey to Jonathon's stupid love games. If Dara's death was somehow connected to Aqua's disappearance, then Jonathon might have some answers. The problem would be getting him to talk.

Luann let out a yelp and then covered her mouth as she stared at Jonathon. Grinning like a wolf, he was waiting for us under the sheets. His bare chest was just as hairy as his head and I covered my mouth too to hold back laughter.

How was I going to do this without losing my cool?

My heart pounded, and my eyes darted to an antique clock on the dresser. The time stuck out as if it had been written in red pen and then circled dozens of times. 26. I knew that number well. It was associated with extreme life events. Usually negative ones. The numbers were trying to speak to me, and they were telling me to leave Jonathon alone. Whatever karma had in store for him, I didn't want to get in the way of it. I took a step back into the sitting area. The number jumped out at me again, this time from a date stamped on a piece of mail on the coffee table. 26.

The message was clear.

I didn't need to wait around for more proof.

The numbers never lied.

"Wait a minute," Jonathon shouted, his smile turning into an expression of utter fury. "Where do you two think you're going?"

"Katie," Luann muttered, frozen in place.

"Change of plans," I blurted out as I grabbed Luann and ran for the exit.

"You'll regret this!" Jonathon shouted. The slamming of his suite door muted the rest of his sentence.

I pushed the button for the elevator repeatedly and tried to keep myself calm. Jonathon was in a horrible mood, and I had no idea how long it would take him to get dressed. When the elevator door dinged, I let out a sigh of relief. I pulled Luann to safety and pressed the button for the lobby.

"What did you do that for?" Luann frowned as the elevator doors closed. "We'll both be fired."

"You still want to work here after what you just saw?" I asked, placing a hand on my hip. "Luann, you can do so much better."

"That's easy for you to say. You actually have brains." Luann folded her arms and sniffled.

"Luann, how often was Dara assigned to clean Jonathon's room?"

"I don't know." She shrugged. "At least once a week. Sometimes two or three times."

"Don't you see what's going on?" I pointed out. "Didn't you hear the things that Jonathon said? He and Dara were hooking up."

"Jonathon and Dara?" Luann raised her eyebrows.

"That's right," I said. "And now she's dead."

The elevator doors opened once they reached the main level. Luann sniffled again and wiped away a tear as she dashed toward the nearest restroom. I ran to follow her, but something blocked my path. My entire torso felt like one giant block of ice. A moment I'd been dreading had arrived.

"Hello, *Katie*." Louie Stone stared right at me and his expression was just as stone-faced as his name. "We need to talk."

Chapter 10

I gulped.

"You have some explaining to do," Louie said. I avoided looking him in the eyes, I felt like he already knew too much.

"I don't mean to be the cause of any conflict among your community," I began. "I know you've found peace in Misty Key, and I don't want to upset that. I'm just looking for my sister."

"Young Miss Aqua. Yes, I know." His voice was raspier than I remembered, but that tended to happen to shifters with age. Their vocal cords were complex—composed of parts that aided him with both human and, in his case, canine communication.

"Then you know that there are bad vibes all over this hotel," I explained. "First my little sister disappears, and then a hotel maid turns up dead. A siren no less."

"And you think the person responsible is targeting magical folk?" His eyes narrowed, and his gray ponytail swung as he nudged me toward a more private spot away from the Carmichaels' elevator. All it took was a few swift movements, and we were standing in the doorway near the back of the Crystal Grande Hotel. "This is one of the few places the security cameras can't see."

"Good." I took a long, calming breath.

"Is this official Seer business?" Louie asked. "I wasn't notified of anything."

"Not exactly." I offered a half-hearted smile.

"Ember, you know better than that." Louie crossed his arms. "Our laws are cut and dry. Misty Key has been a peaceful place for decades. It's one of the few places left that my kind can work as they please alongside other humans."

"I know, and I swear I don't plan on disrupting that," I replied. "I just want to find my sister."

"What does your mother have to say about all of this?" Louie frowned, but it looked more like a scowl.

"She's had dreams," I reported. "Aqua is alive but her time is short. I have to act quickly."

"I see." He looked into my eyes once more as if he were peering straight into my soul. As chief among his clan, he had the rare ability to sense my emotions, much like our family dog. I was sure he felt my need to protect Aqua, and the inner conflict I struggled with regarding my family and my job in the city.

Maybe he sensed even more than that.

"Maybe you can help me," I suggested. "Aqua delivered bread and pastries here every week and sometimes twice a week. I know she spoke with someone here at the hotel every time because the same day she delivered to the hotel, she also put in special requests with Gator at the drugstore. You must have noticed something."

"Most of my work is done outside," he answered. "I saw her a few times in passing, but she spoke to everyone around here. You know how chatty she can be."

"What about your assistant, Thad?"

"What's this got to do with him?" His tone turned argumentative. "Thad did nothing wrong."

I stared at the lines on his face, and for once, Louie broke eye contact.

"Wait a second." I glanced over my shoulder at the touch of a light ocean breeze grazing across my cheek. "Is Thad...is he one of yours?"

"I would appreciate it if you would keep that information to yourself," he muttered. "You're not the only one without updated paperwork." He cleared his throat, his voice sounding even harsher when he whispered. "He's my brother's son, and he's just learned what he is and about the existence of magical species."

"That must have been a nice little reunion."

"My brother is dead," Louie stated plainly. "We lost him on a hunt three years ago."

"I'm sorry to hear that." I bowed my head for a minute as a way of paying my respects to a man I'd only met once as a child.

"Don't be," he responded with little emotion. "We hunt at every full moon, and we have strict rules that aren't to be broken. Of course, my brother had to break protocol."

I processed the story, attempting to match Louie's lack of emotion at the mention of his brother's accident, but I couldn't stop myself from picturing the hunt that happened every full moon and the way the night lit up the swamps. I remembered the howling, and it had been a long time since I'd heard it. I'd ventured out toward the swamps once just to experience it. The sounds were too muffled in the city center.

"Right," I agreed. "I guess your brother had experienced enough hunts to know what he was doing."

"About once a month since he came of age," Louie explained. "Though it all depends on the lunar cycle, but a full moon comes around on a monthly basis, give or take a few days."

"How is Thad adjusting?" I asked. "I mean, has he participated in a hunt yet?"

"One." Louie raised his eyebrows. "I don't care to give any more details than that. It was Friday night, and he's still getting used to the idea."

"Friday was a full moon? That's the night I got here." I tilted my head as I filed the information away in my head.

"Don't your kind believe that destiny is written in the stars or something like that?" he asked.

"Something like that."

"Then I'm sure it was no coincidence." Louie cleared his throat, glancing out the door and back over his shoulder. "I best be going before someone spots us, but you be careful, Ember. It's only a matter of time before the real Katie shows up and folks start asking questions."

"Well, your secret is safe with me if mine is safe with you?"

Louie nodded in agreement as he walked past me and back outside to continue with his chores. My conversation with him had gone better than I'd expected, and I'd gathered more data to think about. My mind ran wild with thoughts and memories until one of them hit me like a sucker punch to the gut.

The lunar cycle.

The dates I'd written down.

Aqua's visits to Gator had been centered on the lunar cycle. They had to be. Gator's records had shown that she'd stopped placing orders for a small period of time toward the end of the month. My heart raced as I thought about it logically. I was confident that if I Iined up all of the dates I would find that Aqua had made her visits to the local drugstore on days leading up to the full moon, with days of little to no activity after the full moon had passed.

If that was true, then I was one step closer to learning the sort of spell that had been cast.

There must have been at least one that required a full moon.

And then there was Dara. I'd found her body on Saturday morning, which meant that she could've died Friday night—the day I'd arrived in Misty Key and the night of the full moon. I clasped my hands together at the thought. I was closer to finding Aqua.

A bloodcurdling scream sent my blood pumping harder.

A burst of adrenaline blasted through my veins as my brain connected the noise with dozens of possibilities, one being that another maid had turned up just like Dara. The scream rang through the hotel again, and this time I was able to deduce that it had come from the lobby.

I jogged toward the source, and I wasn't the only one.

A crowd of people, both guests and staff members, were huddled near the reception desk. Someone yelled that they'd called for an ambulance and Mrs. Carmichael was at the center of the chaos with a hand clutching her chest. She screamed again as she kicked a piece of glass situated on the floor in front of her. I glanced up at the ceiling. The chandelier had fallen, and pieces of it were scattered everywhere.

"Calm down, everyone," Magnus Brown announced to the crowd. "We don't want anyone else getting hurt so if you would all kindly walk carefully toward the nearest exit. And please remember that there is glass on the floor."

The crowd dispersed and left me with a sight I wasn't ready for.

Luann was on her knees crying. Her hands were a ruby red that matched similar stains on her uniform, and next to her was a body. A crimson puddle was situated near his head, and I covered my mouth when I noticed shards of glass stuck in his forehead.

It was Jonathon.

The chandelier had fallen right on top of him.

"No!" Mrs. Carmichael screamed. Magnus held her back, trying to keep her from cutting herself, but Mrs. Carmichael dropped to her knees anyway. "He's alive! I know he's alive! Where is that dadgum ambulance?"

Luann covered her face as tears flowed down her cheeks. I tiptoed toward the scene to console her, but I stopped when I noticed a number flashing on the elevator in the main lobby. It was stuck on the fourth floor. I balled my hands into fists and checked the time on a grandfather clock near the reception desk. *Another seven.* In a peculiar pattern near Jonathon's body, droplets of blood formed the same number. *Seven.*

The wailing of a siren came closer and closer until finally, the front doors flew open and a team of medical professionals took over. One of them led Luann and me outside for some fresh air. I rubbed my eyes again and again—another number jumping out at me, this time on the ambulance that had just arrived. *Vehicle Seven.*

"Excuse us," a voice shouted as a stretcher was wheeled out of the hotel in a matter of minutes.

"My baby," Mrs. Carmichael shouted as she followed them and stepped into the ambulance. "Please, save my baby!"

The doors slammed shut, and the ambulance sped back toward town.

The fact that Jonathon hadn't left in a body bag meant that he was still alive.

"What happened?" I felt a tap on my shoulder and all at once every guest and employee at the hotel seemed to break out in incessant chatter. Louie looked straight at me waiting for a clear response. "I heard the screams and the ambulance. Who did they come for?"

"Jonathon." I gulped. I couldn't hide the worried look in my eyes, especially not from Louie

Stone. A killer walked the grounds of the Crystal Grande Hotel—a ruthless one.

"Who?" Louie muttered as if sniffing out my fears.

"A witch," I replied. "And let's hope that there is only *one*."

Chapter 11

Monday morning brought with it mixed emotions and a whole lot of speculating. I'd lain awake all night answering work emails, not able to concentrate on much. I couldn't get the sight of Jonathon unconscious under a heap of broken glass out of my head. I'd checked the news multiple times throughout the night, knowing that Jonathon's death would be front page material. So far, I hadn't found anything new posted about the Carmichael family. Most of the staff had been so traumatized by the event that Magnus had given half of the maids, including me, some time off.

Yogi trotted into my bedroom and let out a quiet bark. I knew that meant that a new copy of the *Misty Messenger* was waiting on the doorstep. I closed my eyes as I formulated one more email in my head. It was the email I had to send to Mr. Cohen explaining that I was going to need more time off. The vacation days weren't a problem. I hadn't taken a vacation since I'd gotten the job. It was the owner's visit at the end of the week that worried me. I had to be there.

I opened my message with a few sentences about my current family situation.

My little sister is missing, and my mother isn't doing so well...

I shook my head and deleted it.

I have family business to attend to that has taken me longer than expected. Not to worry. I will be back in my office bright and early...

I paused and took a deep breath as Stevie knocked on the door. She raised her eyebrows, glaring at my phone. I quickly saved my email and tossed it aside. Stevie was wearing her usual T-shirt and shorts, and her apron from the bakery was hanging over her shoulder. She held a mug bearing the word *cattitude* in one hand and leaned against the doorframe.

"Mom is watching the bakery for a bit," she said. "Orion is at school. I thought I would check on you and see how you slept last night." She took a sip from her mug as she studied me. "It seems like the entire town is on edge waiting to hear about Jonathon Carmichael. I've heard my fair share of theories in the bakery this morning."

"What's the buzz?" I asked.

"Some say it was an accident," Stevie replied. "And some say attempted murder."

"I still say witches."

"I hope you're full of it." Stevie made a sour face as soon as my prediction left my lips.

"What do you have against witches anyway?"

"Nothing." Stevie frowned, staring down at her coffee. "Besides, what do you care? As soon as Aqua is home you're off to NYC again."

I rolled my eyes. "You would be even more offended if I stayed and started tweaking things at the shop."

"At least I would have a sister around to yell at." The phone rang, and Yogi barked along with it. "Thank the cosmos. I'll get that."

The second Stevie left, I grabbed my phone again. Yogi trotted upstairs and nudged the side of my leg before returning to the doorway. He wagged his tail when I began to follow him back down the staircase and into the kitchen where Stevie stood looking concerned.

"What is it?" I asked as soon as Stevie hung up. "Is it Jonathon?"

"Nope." Stevie shook her head. "It's Dara. Her ma is at the bakery, and she wants to talk to you."

"Me?" I pointed to myself, wondering what the woman might want. Details? Closure? Some sort of explanation as to what might have happened to her daughter? Whatever it was, it was sure to be an uncomfortable conversation.

"Yeah, you," Stevie responded. "She probably just wants a reading. I can't give her one and neither can Ma. Get dressed. We're going for a walk."

After I changed into the only non-professional outfit I had, Stevie, Yogi, and I walked toward Main Street. It was another humid morning much like yesterday, and I was already too warm in my yoga pants. The scent of baked goods lingered in the air as soon as Lunar Bakery was in sight. The *Open* sign glowed in the window and Stevie's new special, *Healing Hummingbird Bars*, was written on a chalkboard outside. I smiled, seeing that the door was propped open to accommodate all of the customers in line. The bakery was constantly busy, and my sister was obviously worn out and overstressed. She needed to hire some help.

She needed me to work my magic just as much as Aqua did.

I took a deep breath and pushed those thoughts away.

One problem at a time. Focus on one problem at a time.

Stevie tied her apron as she approached the bakery. Yogi walked through the front door like he owned the place, and several customers scowled at me as I cut through the line. I held up my hands in surrender, letting them know I wasn't butting my way up to the front.

"Finally," Mom muttered when she saw us. "Thank you and have a stellar day, sir." My mom looked neatly put together, which was a refreshing sight, and her moonstone sparkled in the rays of sunshine filling the front windows. She pointed to a table in the corner where a dark-haired woman resembling Dara sat quietly with a cup of coffee. "Ellen is waiting over there. Help me out, will you, Stevie?"

"It's what I do best," she replied, glancing in my direction.

Stevie assisted my mom at the register as I cautiously approached the woman who was waiting for me. Yogi stayed at my side and even sniffed out the chair opposite the woman before I sat down. I forced a smile, expecting a burst of tears or a fragile look of hope.

Dara's mother saw me and frowned.

"Hi, I'm Ember. You must be Ellen. I don't know what my mother told you, but I don't do readings at the moment." I held out a hand, but she didn't return the friendly gesture.

"Are you the one who found my Dara?" Ellen asked. The ends of her hair were ratty, and there were bags under her eyes suggesting that she hadn't slept in days. "I've been looking everywhere for the maid that was with Luann when she found my daughter. She seems to think your name is Katie, but I know better. I went to find this Katie girl at the hotel yesterday, and someone pointed at you. I've known your mother since you and your sisters were babies. A pair of glasses wasn't enough to fool me."

I gulped. I hadn't been expecting her to say that.

"So you reported me to the manager?"

"No," she replied. "I'm here to make a deal. Since you're a Seer, I'll give you the benefit of the doubt. Your organization has always been good to me. I'm sure you have a good reason for doing...whatever it is that you're doing. I just want some answers."

"As do I," I said quietly.

"You tell me everything you know about my daughter's death, and I won't tell Mrs. Carmichael that one of her maids is an imposter."

"Fair enough," I agreed. "Yes, I did find Dara Saturday morning. It was my first day at the Crystal Grande, and I was helping Luann clean rooms."

"The police say it was cardiac arrest, but Dara was in good health," Ellen added. "What do you think?"

"I think there are a number of things that could've happened." My eyes darted to the clock on the wall, the menu board, and the table next to us, searching for anything with numbers or patterns that might help me.

"I'm asking you what *you* think," Ellen clarified with a stern look on her face.

Back when I had my Seer license, I tried to read the numbers in moments like these. It was sometimes hard to distinguish a person's true motives. Was Ellen out for closure or revenge? Did she really intend to report me to the authorities or had she been looking for someone to sucker into doing her bidding?

I squinted at the menu on the wall near the register. This was the part of the job I hated. My readings had never been consistent, and I'd never known why. I glanced at the time on my phone and focused as best as I could. Nothing.

"I think it was an unfortunate accident," I answered after a few failed attempts to get a read on Ellen.

"And?" Her eyes went wide.

"And it shouldn't have happened," I continued.

"That's not good enough," she rudely remarked. She flipped a strand of tangled hair over her shoulder. "I take it you knew what Dara was. It's tradition for a siren to pass her talent along to another family member when she passes away. We gather together and perform a special ceremony. I inherited mine from my grandmother. It's a beautiful custom that sirens have carried on for centuries. But Dara had no talent to give."

"What do you mean?" I leaned in closer, the wheels in my head turning. Yogi's ears perked up too.

"I mean we performed the ceremony, and nothing happened," she said through her teeth as if it were my fault. "It's like all of Dara's talents were taken from her, but I've never heard of such a thing."

"Me neither," I agreed.

"Well?" Ellen impatiently tapped her fingers on the table, glaring at me with the harshest of looks. "What do the Clairs plan on doing about it?"

"Oh." I took a deep breath, wondering how I could politely answer her question in a manner that she would be satisfied with. I couldn't think of anything off the top of my head, and Ellen seemed like the type of woman who might cause a scene. "Normally, you submit your case, and then a Seer or a team of Seers are assigned to your case."

"I've already done that," she responded. "There's a waiting list. Apparently, they don't have sufficient personnel in my area to work my case right away." She raised her eyebrows again.

She did think this was my fault.

"I'm sure you won't have to wait much longer," I lied.

"You know, I thought psychics were supposed to be insightful, peaceful people." Ellen stood up angrily, and Yogi was quick to position himself in between her and me. "That's not the impression I got when I contacted your regional representative. If this is the sort of service to be expected nowadays, what's the purpose of even dealing with psychics anymore? At least the frauds that hold readings in trailer parks with cheap crystal balls give people straight answers."

Ellen stormed off and turned heads as she went. I was left sitting at the quaint café table speechless. I had some idea what Ellen was going through, losing a loved one and having so many unanswered questions. The Clairs had frustrated me as well, telling me that I was in control of my gift when I clearly wasn't. The numbers seemed to speak to me only when they wanted to. I couldn't even get the slightest reading off of Ellen.

I stared down at the wooden table, processing my meeting with Dara's mother. Dara had been a siren, but by the time she'd died, she didn't give off any magical energy. There were no signs suggesting that she wasn't human. And there was the full moon and the fact that Aqua's visits to Gator lined up with the lunar cycle. There was also the attempt on Jonathon Carmichael's life. He must have known something about Dara that he shouldn't have. Everything was linked somehow.

I knew for certain that there was a witch residing in Misty Key, and she was up to something.

There was another way I could figure out what, but Stevie was going to hate it.

Yogi bumped my leg, and I looked up just in time to see a face that made me roll my eyes. Nova bounced when she walked, holding a leather messenger bag as she strode to the front of the line with a grin of importance. A few customers whispered as she passed them but Nova didn't seem to mind. She cut to the front of the line and leaned over the counter, saying something to my mother that I couldn't make out. A minute later Nova was at my table making herself comfortable. Yogi barked at the sight of her and I figured the bark was meant for the Siamese ghost cat that acted as her *dead* companion.

"There you are," Nova said as she placed her messenger bag on her lap and pulled out a folder stuffed with papers. She paused to sniff the air and make sure that every strand of her auburn hair was in place. "I was just telling your mother that the Clairs have decided to investigate your sister's disappearance. I would put you and your sister on the case, but unfortunately, your license is expired. As you know, that makes things difficult."

"It has for years," I muttered.

"Do you have your paperwork?" she asked. "I can fast-track your renewal. Of course, you will have to take your Seer test again, but a couple of readings is hardly a big deal."

"That depends on the day," I responded.

Nova narrowed her eyes and studied my expression. She tilted her head and then took a deep breath. I had yet to discover what Nova's gift was but I had the gut feeling that I would soon find out. There were ways to block psychic-to-psychic readings and predictions, but I wasn't well practiced in any of them.

"Ember, will you go grab me something up front?" Nova asked.

"Is this some sort of test?" I questioned her. "If it is, now is not the time."

"No." Nova shook her head. "But I think you need some advice, and I just want to help."

"I appreciate the offer Nova, but—"

"Just go and get me something," she repeated. "I promise you won't be sorry." She paused and cleared her throat. "And whether or not you trust in my reading, at least you'll get to see what category of clairs my gift falls under."

"Stevie has made that into a guessing game." I shrugged. "All right. What do you want?"

"You pick," Nova replied.

Yogi followed me as I walked behind the busy counter. I ignored the looks of confusion from both Stevie and my mom as I grabbed a clean plate and observed the available pastries that were on display. Stevie brushed against my arm as she reached behind me to grab a loaf of honey wheat bread for a customer.

My eyes were drawn to the pound cakes first, and not because they were my favorite. Stevie made three flavors every day and cut them into thick slices. Today's flavors were classic vanilla, cherry almond, and banana nut. The vanilla slices were almost gone, but the banana nut pound cake was the most abundant item on the menu. My first instinct was to take a slice to Nova.

My eyes then darted to the item that seemed to be running low. Stevie reached in front of me, shooting me a strange look again as she packaged up four pecan sticky buns. The sugary scent and crisp, golden edges of the pastries were enough to make my mouth water. I took another whiff of them and then quickly grabbed one of the few that were left.

I carefully placed the plate in front of Nova, figuring that she might as well try a bestseller her first time eating at the Lunar Bakery. I sat down opposite her and watched as she took a minute to smell the sweet pecan roll. She touched the warm glaze on top and studied the golden-brown edges. Finally, she took a bite and stared off at nothing as she chewed. For a moment I wondered if she was in a trance, but then her gaze fell to me, and I knew that she'd gathered some insights into my life.

I leaned back in my chair and folded my arms. Stevie was going to get a kick out of what I'd just discovered. Our psychic gifts manifested in many different forms but most fell under the umbrella of the six clairs. I'd read about Nova's gift before, but she was the first Seer I'd ever seen use it in person.

Clairvoyance was the most popular gift, and it mostly consisted of interpreting someone's present and future through symbols. There was clairsentience, which was the gift of the empath. Clairaudience and claircognizance consisted of hearing and knowing someone's present and future through intuition. Clairalience was the least favored because it consisted of reading a person based on smell. And then there was Nova's gift—the ability to read someone using taste.

"Clairgustance," I stated as I watched her at work. "That's a sight I thought I'd never see."

"Food can be very telling, Ember." Nova swallowed her first bite and nodded. "Everything about the way a person connects with food can be interpreted. I can taste how stressed your whole family is."

"My sister is missing," I pointed out. "Obviously, we're all stressed about it."

"Okay, well then let me point out some less obvious things, like your dilemma in renewing your Seer license." She raised her eyebrows. "I can't quite put my finger on everything, but I sense a lack of faith on your part."

"Excuse me?" I didn't understand what she was getting at. "What does *faith* have to do with anything?"

"It's everything," Nova explained. "How can others put their faith in you when you have no faith in yourself?" She touched another section of the sticky bun and took another tiny bite as she contemplated some more. "You're not a fan of sugar-coating, so I'll cut to the chase."

"Please do." I did my best to remain polite, but I wasn't sure what to expect from Nova. Her reading hadn't given me any insights so far, and there was no way I was going to tell her the secret that had been weighing on my chest since my dad had died.

"I read your file," she admitted. "You've had some trouble harnessing your gift."

"I guess Lady Deja's advice just didn't resonate with me."

"You were making slow and steady progress before in controlling your talent, but then something changed after your father died." She observed my expression. "Now you've lost your sense of identity, which is why your gift only seems to appear when your emotions spike. That's a start, but you can't rely on emotionally driven information. It's better to remain calm when life throws us curve balls."

"I know perfectly well who I am," I responded. "Ask anyone at Fillmore Media. I'm very good at what I do." I was back to showcasing my firing face—little-to-no emotion and the appearance of utmost professionalism.

"What you *do* is not who you are," Nova clarified. "You have some dire decisions to make."

"Yes, I know." I nodded in agreement.

"It has been over a hundred years since a psychic has had her gifts wiped clean," Nova said. "I don't want you to be next. Your family's magical line would start to die out, not to mention the nasty side effects that ended up driving the last woman insane. Our abilities make up part of our souls, and souls can't go broken without serious consequences."

"I know the consequences, and I also know that Lady Deja refuses to perform cleansings for that very reason," I said. "I read up on it once. At worst, she'll just erase my knowledge of the Clairs' inner workings and bind my talents for a while. I'm familiar with the amendments she made to our laws last year."

"Well, at least you're current on *something*. I'm going to put Stevie on the case and make you her assistant." Nova pulled out a form and began jotting things down. "You two will have every resource at your disposal to find Aqua."

"You want me to play intern?" I shook my head. "I'm sorry, Nova, but I'm being pulled in too many directions. I don't even know how much longer I can stay in Misty Key. I have a very important meeting I need to be at on Friday."

"I know," she stated, not looking the least bit sympathetic. "Whether or not you comply with my request is up to you. No one is forcing you to serve the magical community. But when you do, you should give it everything you've got."

Nova pushed aside the rest of her pecan sticky bun and stood up to leave. She placed a form on the table that gave Stevie and me official permission to investigate. Stevie would be pleased, but I had some more thinking to do. At the moment, my top priority was finding my sister so I could return to New York City.

"According to my file, *everything I've got* isn't much," I commented.

Nova shrugged. "That can change if you want it to."

She left the bakery the way she'd entered— with a grin of importance and, judging from Yogi's odd behavior, the ghost of a cat trailing behind her.

Chapter 12

"Clairgustance?"

Stevie threw her head back and practically cackled. She'd been having trouble sitting still since the moment I'd told her about Nova's gift. My mother served us all her usual sweet chicken salad with croissants and the leftover banana nut pound cake. Orion grinned as he took a heaping bite of his sandwich.

"That's right," I responded.

"I thought that gift was a joke the first time I heard about it." Stevie laughed again. "No wonder she acted a little weird that day she came over. Who knows what kind of impressions she got about us when she tasted that cheddar croissant."

"The good news is that the Clairs have given us their blessing." My mom poured herself another glass of sweet tea. It had been a busy day at the bakery, but Stevie hadn't let me do much to help her.

"And a chance for Ember to renew her license," Stevie added.

"Don't call me your assistant," I replied.

Orion giggled.

"Fine." She poured a glass of sweet tea and slid it toward me. "Drink this and I'll respect your wishes."

"What's wrong with it?" I looked into the cup. The cool, amber liquid appeared to be fine, but I never knew what Stevie had up her sleeve.

"Nothing." Stevie smirked. "I haven't seen you drink any sweet tea since you've been here. It used to be your favorite."

"No, it used to be my only option because Mom wouldn't let us drink coffee."

"Drink it then," Stevie insisted.

I rolled my eyes and took a gulp of sweet tea. It tasted the way I'd remembered it, and it pushed thoughts of our childhood to the forefront of my brain. I hadn't realized how long I'd gone without it. Since I'd moved to the city, coffee had replaced most of my cravings. Sweet tea wasn't readily available at most restaurants I went to. I smiled.

"Tastes like high school," I stated.

My mom and Stevie laughed, and for once sitting at the kitchen table with my family brought back pleasant memories—ones that I'd let go of for some reason. Mom's smile was warm as she tugged on her moonstone. I was relieved to see her without tears in her eyes. She also appeared to be sleeping a little better.

"Can you tell me my future now?" Stevie joked.

"I see you meeting a nice young man," I answered, mimicking Nova's overly proper mannerisms. "A southern gentleman who attends church every Sunday and never forgets to floss."

My mom, Stevie, and Orion broke out in laughter.

"*Mom* going to church?" Orion said in between giggles. "That's a good one, Auntie Ember."

"Oh, what a treat it is to see my girls back together again." My mom took a deep breath as the laughing died down and the memory of Aqua's dire situation sunk back in.

"Soon there will be three of us." Stevie nodded reassuringly. "What was it you wanted to say, Ember?"

"Yes," I responded. "I think I know how to figure out the identity of this mystery witch." I braced myself for an argument. Although I'd made progress in investigating Aqua's disappearance, my next suggestion was going to make Stevie mad.

"How?" Stevie eagerly awaited my explanation.

"First let me tell you what I know." I'd reasoned that if I could make Stevie understand my next request, she might not reject it on the spot. "A witch is behind Aqua's disappearance, Dara's death, and Jonathon's accident. We know that Aqua was making purchases for someone at the Crystal Grande and these purchases seem to coincide with the lunar cycle. Dara died the night of a full moon, and Jonathon had closer ties to Dara than any of us had thought."

"Ew." Stevie rolled her eyes. "Dara could've done much better."

"So the question is why?" I continued. "Why kidnap someone and kill another?"

"*Total world domination,*" Orion sang as if the four of us were living out one of the plots in his comic books.

"Power," Stevie chimed in. "Isn't that all spellcasters care about? If it weren't for our treaty with Wisteria, Inc., they would be trying to rule the magical world and the human one."

"All the more reason to try and figure out what this witch is looking for," I added. "We have information now that might help us identify the type of potion this witch made."

"Oh, no." Stevie shook her head. "No. No. No. I won't do it."

"But if we can identify the potion and the spell, we'll be one step ahead of—"

"No way," Stevie continued. "I can't believe you would even suggest it."

"What am I missing here?" my mom asked. She furrowed her brow as she watched Stevie pace up and down the kitchen.

"Stevie is scared of a little field trip."

"Scared?" Stevie rolled her eyes. "You're kidding me, right? I see ghosts on a daily basis. I can handle a spellcaster. But a whole family of them..."

"Oh, I see." My mom took a deep breath. "You want to visit Dr. and Mrs. Grant. They live up north in Cottonberry now. The trip will take you all day."

"I'm aware of that, Ma," Stevie muttered.

"I'll mind the bakery," Mom volunteered. "Visiting the Grants is a two-woman job."

"As the only family of witches and warlocks around, they are our only hope of learning more about what's going on at the Crystal Grande. They might even have a remedy for that binding spell on Dara's spirit. You would finally be able to make contact with her. If you won't do it for any other reason, do it for Aqua."

Stevie stopped her pacing and rubbed the side of her forehead. She cleared her throat and ran her fingers over the sleeve of tattoos on her arm, stopping at one in particular near her elbow. I knew that she had some unresolved issues with the Grants, one Grant in particular, but I hoped that my plea would be enough.

"Okay, we'll go tomorrow." Stevie closed her eyes and then grabbed her plate and walked straight upstairs to her room.

* * *

It seemed to be a pattern in my life that when one area was thriving, another was dying. Monday night was no exception. I searched through my suitcase for a suitable outfit for the morning. We would have to start our drive to Cottonberry bright and early to make it there by lunchtime. There would be plenty to see and do once we arrived, but the drive was sure to be exhausting. And possibly silent depending on Stevie's mood.

Yogi sat at the foot of my bed as I changed into my pajamas and sat down to answer more emails. The things Nova had said to me stirred in my head, and I found myself looking for reasons why she was wrong about me. I couldn't think of many.

My eyes went wide when I came across an email from my boss, Mr. Cohen.

He'd given one of my clients to someone else, and he only did that when he was upset. I quickly glanced at the time, accounted for the time difference, and determined that Mr. Cohen might still be in his office prepping for the owner's visit at the end of the week. I nervously dialed his number, my heart pounding so fiercely that I heard a ringing through my ears.

"Mr. Cohen's office," a familiar voice answered.

"Erica?" I responded.

"Yes?" she sounded confused.

"Is Mr. Cohen in his office?" I asked.

"Yes?" Erica still sounded a little dumbfounded by the whole conversation.

"Put me through," I instructed her.

"Oh, I can't just—"

"Yes, you can," I interrupted. "Just put me through, or I'll call him on his cell and tell him that you refused to let him speak to his top colleague."

"Oh, it's you, Ms. Greene," Erica finally said. "I thought your voice sounded familiar." I imagined her in one of her usual loud outfits chewing a gob of gum as she worked. "Mr. Cohen has me floating around the office until you get back."

"Hopefully, it won't be much longer," I replied.

"Yeah, of course, Ms. Greene." She let out a polite laugh. "Let me put you th—"

Before she had the chance to finish her sentence, the phone rang, and Mr. Cohen answered.

"Ember, I was beginning to get worried," he replied.

"No need for that," I assured him. "I'll be there for Mr. Fillmore on Friday."

"So, you've finally booked that flight." He coughed and paused for a minute to take a drink, which he had no problem vocalizing over the phone.

"Ahhh. Now that's what I call whiskey. Do they drink whiskey down in the boonies?"

"They prefer their moonshine," I sarcastically answered.

"Hilarious." His hoarse chuckle sounded less like a laugh and more like an avid smoker trying to catch a breath.

"I don't know for sure what day I'll be back, but—"

"Whoa," he butted in. "Wait a minute. You gave me your word that you would be in yesterday and I've been patient with you."

"It's a family emergency."

"I understand that," he continued. "But your work family is about to have an emergency as well if you don't get back here before Friday. Video conferencing just isn't the same thing as offering information in person. Now, I'm just trying to look out for your best interest."

"I understand," I responded.

"We're very pleased with the work you've done this year but..." He paused and exhaled loudly into the receiver. "I'm not supposed to say this, Ember, but you've left me with no choice." He cleared his scratchy throat and took another swig of whiskey. It must have been the fuel that kept his fire burning until his work was finished for the evening.

"I'm listening." I clutched my phone tighter than I meant to and my fingers felt like they were stuck stiffly in place.

"Mr. Fillmore has you in mind for that open director position, but he's made it clear that he's awarding that promotion in person. If you're not here, he'll give it to Charles."

"Shoot," I murmured. "*Aries*. It's always the Arieses."

"What?"

"Nothing," I answered.

"Call me when you've booked that flight," Mr. Cohen reiterated. "Otherwise, you might be coming home to an office down the hall from the newest Director of Finance. Please tell me that you get it, kid."

"I get it."

I clenched my hands into fists the second I hung up. I wanted to scream into my pillow and pack my bags. The decisions I'd been faced with lately hadn't been easy ones, and this one was the worst—the mother of all tipping points.

I had to choose between my new life and my old one.

And I had to choose soon.

Chapter 13

The heat didn't disappear the farther we drove from the coast. If anything, it got worse. Stevie had insisted on driving, and I succumbed to whatever would make her feel most comfortable. She'd gone back and forth between blasting the air conditioner and rolling down her windows. This was mostly because her air conditioner didn't work half the time and it was overheating her engine.

"Five miles to Cottonberry," Stevie announced. She'd said little the whole drive. "*Effin'* Cottonberry."

"It's an okay town," I admitted. "There's the college."

"I know it well," Stevie replied. "And I doubt they'll ever let me back in that place."

"You weren't that bad," I argued.

"Easy for you to say, Miss Straight A's," Stevie muttered to herself as she steered toward the exit.

Cottonberry was close to the Georgia border, and it housed one of the best universities in the state. It was a town with classic southern charm and a rich history. The air wasn't as crisp since the ocean wasn't nearby. I wiped a bead of sweat from my forehead and rolled down my window as Stevie turned onto the main road that went right in front of the college and the little lane of shops across the street. Her air conditioner was acting up again.

The trees were still green, and the sidewalks buzzed with students. I watched as we passed the administrative building with its dark red bricks and a clock overlooking campus. It was just as dignified and magnificent-looking as I remembered. The shops across the street were just as inviting and most of them hadn't changed. Stevie quickly pulled into an open parking spot and turned off the car.

"Are you okay?" I asked. "The Grants live ten minutes away. Why are we stopping?"

"Because I need...an ice cream." She grabbed her purse and jumped out of the car.

"No, you're just nervous," I observed. She hung the strap of her purse over her shoulder and clutched it tightly. I knew this was hard for her but the sooner we visited the Grants, the sooner we could head back to Misty Key.

"Fine, I'm just nervous." Stevie ran her fingers through her dark bob.

"Why?" I asked. "It's not like the Grants will even remember us. We're showing up on their doorstep on official Seer business, remember?"

"I was hoping it wouldn't come to this, but there's something you should know," she confessed. She cleared her throat, avoiding eye contact. "The

Grants *will* remember me. I dated their son." She wrinkled her nose like she'd just smelled something grotesque.

"Which one?" I placed a hand on my hip, shocked that Stevie would even toy with the idea of dating a spellcaster, let alone kiss one.

"That's not important." Stevie nodded and exhaled loudly. "Man, it feels good to get that off my chest."

"Anything else?" I raised my eyebrows.

"Yeah," she responded. "If Mrs. Grant says anything weird, just don't listen, okay? This all happened a really long time ago."

"You got it." I chuckled to myself as I hopped back in the car and waited for Stevie to work up the nerve to finish our long drive.

Just past campus were grandiose neighborhoods with historic homes. My eyes widened with every manicured lawn and giant front porch. Stevie slowed down as we approached one of the largest homes on the street. It was a white Georgian home with gray shutters that framed every window. A staircase led to a porch with massive columns and an outdoor sitting area that looked too perfect to disturb. It was truly something out of a magazine.

"Dang," Stevie breathed as she parked in the driveway. "I guess they're still doing well."

"Extremely."

"So much for voodoo," Stevie muttered as she jumped out and jogged up the staircase. Her finger froze just before ringing the doorbell.

I gave Stevie a minute to collect her thoughts and wiped another bead of sweat from my forehead. I hadn't looked in a mirror since breakfast, and the drive had been a little rough. I licked my lips and rubbed underneath my lower lashes, hoping to catch any drippy mascara. I'd been tired of walking everywhere in yoga pants, so I'd opted to wear my usual clothes.

My blouse and pencil skirt were a stark contrast to Stevie's normal attire. I quickly stepped in front of her as I reached out to ring the doorbell myself. Stevie didn't seem to mind. In fact, she gave me her signal of approval by taking a step backward. This meant that it was up to me to do the talking. The front double doors opened, and I tilted my head upon seeing Mrs. Grant. I'd expected a maid or even a butler to answer. Maybe the Grants hadn't been doing as well as Stevie had thought.

"Hello, my name is Ember, and we're here on behalf of the Clairs," I recited. My prior training was all coming back to me.

"Oh." Mrs. Grant sighed as she opened the door further. "I suppose I have to let you in then."

I entered the foyer, and Mrs. Grant raised her eyebrows as Stevie walked inside behind me. She glared at Stevie's outfit as if a hard stare might make her jean shorts and T-shirt turn into a fancy cocktail dress. I cleared my throat, hoping to keep her attention away from my sister.

"I'm sorry," I stated. "What's your first name?"

"Irrelevant," she answered. Mrs. Grant's hair shimmered a deep red under the light. She was petite, but her face was round with rosy cheeks. She wore high heels and beige slacks that had been perfectly pressed. Her slacks represented the rest of her home—white, flawless, and expensive. "The treaty says I must cooperate, so what is it that you want?"

"Who is it, dear?" a voice called from the other room. Judging from its masculinity, I concluded that it must be Dr. Grant.

"Just some fortune tellers, or whatever it is they call themselves," she shouted back.

"No manners," Stevie murmured.

"Wait a minute." Mrs. Grant pointed at Stevie. "I thought I recognized you. Well, bless your little heart, you're that girl from the bakery."

"I have a name, but you never used it back then," Stevie answered, forcing a polite smile. "Why bother now?"

"Earle, get in here," Mrs. Grant called to her husband. "You've got to see this."

"*Oh, kill me now,*" Stevie muttered under her breath.

Dr. Grant entered the foyer wearing a red smoking jacket. Stevie rolled her eyes when she saw him. I covered my mouth as a look of surprise crossed his face. Dr. and Mrs. Grant exchanged a few hushed comments before looking Stevie up and down in disbelief.

"Well, I never thought I'd see the day," Dr. Grant stated. "I see you haven't changed much."

"Likewise." Stevie clenched her jaw, glaring at me.

"Yes, it's crazy," I blurted out. "Anyway—"

"I mean, to think that our son ever dated you," Mrs. Grant added, looking wide-eyed at her husband. "I'm glad he grew out of his little rebellious phase." She sported a twisted smile as if dating Stevie were the same as collecting baseball cards at age twelve.

"So glad," Dr. Grant chimed in with a chuckle.

"And this from a man wearing velvet," Stevie stated with a smile.

"As I was saying." I raised my voice, realizing that it would take much more energy than I'd accounted for to dominate the conversation. "We're here on official Seer business, and we need to ask you a few questions." I pulled a piece of paper from my pocket on which I'd written down all of the ingredients Aqua had purchased from Gator before she'd gone missing. "Can you please tell me what these items are commonly used for?"

"Let's see." Mrs. Grant grabbed the paper and squinted. "Oh, I can't see a darn thing. Oh, you read it, Earle."

"Lemongrass, lavender, hawthorn berries, red pepper, bauhinia flowers," he listed off. "Deer tongue. That's interesting."

"We'll have to check the book," Mrs. Grant commented. "These can be used for a number of spells and potions."

"Ah, just a minute, dear." Earle pulled out his cell phone and began typing. "Warner loaded everything onto the computer, remember? I can search through the database on my phone."

"Yes, that's right." She waved her hand proudly. "Our Warner is so smart. You know he's married now to a lovely young witch from Birmingham. We just adore her, don't we, Earle?"

"Indeed," her husband agreed while keeping his nose buried in his phone.

"She's a fabulous cook," Mrs. Grant went on. "Just magical in the kitchen."

"And a witch everywhere else?" Stevie added quietly.

"I've got a few matches." Dr. Grant held up his finger. "Okay, lemongrass and lavender are used in revival potions when someone falls ill. Hawthorn berries are used for things like astral projection—

separating the mind and the body. Red pepper is a popular binder that keeps spirits from talking, and bauhinia flowers are commonly used in protection potions."

"So none of them are used all together?" I asked.

"No." Dr. Grant nodded matter-of-factly.

"Do any of those spells require a full moon?" I continued.

"No." Dr. Grant reread his search results a second time.

"Shoot." I took a deep breath. "And there's no way all of those ingredients could be used to make some sort of hybrid-type potion?"

"A *hybrid* potion?" Mrs. Grant threw her head back and let out a giggle. "Did you hear that, Earle? Bless her heart. Spell-blending is forbidden. Everyone knows that."

"Why?" I looked from Mrs. Grant to her husband, Earle.

"Because of the serious repercussions," Dr. Grant explained. "A young witch tried it once back when my great-grandmother was a child. It was so horrible that Wisteria, Inc., banned spell-blending with a unanimous vote."

"What happened?" Stevie curiously inquired.

"She wouldn't give me the details," Dr. Grant replied. "Although she might have told you two on behalf of the treaty. She always did have a soft spot for fortune tellers."

"Seers," Stevie corrected him.

"Anyway." He cleared his throat, placing his phone back in his pocket. "She's dead. Is that all you need?"

"No." Stevie boldly stepped forward, taking control of the conversation. I crossed my arms and watched in amazement as she managed to smile and speak as if she hadn't been the least bit offended by the comments the Grants had made about her.

Maybe it was a trap.

"Sorry, honey, I can't give you Warner's phone number," Mrs. Grant explained. "Like I said, he's a married man, and I don't want you ruining everything."

My heart pounded as I studied Stevie's reaction. Mrs. Grant had practically called her a home-wrecker before she'd even explained what she wanted. I did my best to steady my breathing, but the anticipation flooded my veins with anxiety. Why wasn't Stevie upset?

"Mrs. Grant," Stevie stated politely, "I want your son's phone number just as much as I want to dress up in a sparkly, pink gown and audition for a beauty pageant. Now, the two of you are just as bigoted and shallow as you were when I was a teen." She turned her attention to Dr. Grant. "I would prefer to speak to your dead great-granny. Where is she buried, please?"

"The churchyard near campus," Dr. Grant answered. "Most of my family is buried here in Cottonberry."

"And her name?" Stevie raised her eyebrows, seemingly pleased with the look of confusion on Mrs. Grant's face.

"Muriel Grant," he said.

"Thank you." Stevie nodded and turned to leave.

"But you can't contact her spirit, I'm afraid," Mrs. Grant blurted out. "We conjure a graveyard ghoul every year to guard our relatives and ensure that they rest in peace. He'll rip you to pieces if you try anything."

"I'll take my chances," Stevie responded.

"Can't you give him the night off or something?" I suggested.

"No," Mrs. Grant answered with a twisted smile. "Once he's conjured, he only has one purpose. No exceptions. Sorry, dears."

I clenched my jaw as I followed Stevie back to her car. The Grants stood on their front porch and watched us every step of the way. Mrs. Grant frowned as if she expected Stevie to steal an item of patio furniture on her way out. I hopped in the passenger's seat, and Stevie started the engine.

Before she drove away, Stevie leaned out her window.

"By the way, you're not a doctor," Stevie yelled. "You have a PhD in something no one cares about! And your son is lousy with his broomstick, if you know what I mean!"

The two of us laughed as we drove away, and I could've sworn I heard Mrs. Grant cursing as we sped down the street.

* * *

I walked reverently through the cemetery as Stevie read each headstone aloud. We'd stopped for food before deciding to contact Muriel Grant in hopes of learning what had happened when she was a kid. I clasped my hands together, feeling out of place. Stevie looked completely comfortable and even at peace with herself. A permanent smile was ingrained on her face, and every once in a while, she chuckled. I'd gathered from observing her that people became much more comical once they were dead.

"You didn't really sleep with Warner Grant, did you?"

"What do you think?" Stevie read off another name and continued walking.

"I don't know what to think. That's why I'm asking."

"Of course I didn't," Stevie clarified. "We barely even made it to date number three before I couldn't stand him anymore. I was just trying to make Mrs. Grant mad."

"You succeeded," I said. "I'm surprised she hasn't sicced her ghoul on us yet."

"You and me both," Stevie agreed.

The cemetery had a nice view of a stone chapel, and it sat next to a thick grove of forest trees. A church bell rang, letting us know darkness was approaching, and gray clouds overhead provided cooler evening air. I was grateful that it wasn't as hot as it had been during the day. The sweat stains on my blouse weren't flattering at all, and I was getting tired of keeping my face moisture free.

The lawn was neatly manicured, and many headstones had been decorated with fresh flowers of every variety. Stevie pointed to a headstone up ahead. It was the tallest one around, and it had recently been graced with an exquisite wreath of roses. Stevie grinned as she read Muriel's name out loud.

"There she is," I muttered.

"We should have walked straight toward the biggest and most expensive-looking ones right when we got here." Stevie gently touched the headstone. "Why didn't I think of that before?"

"It's a beautiful wreath," I added.

"I'm sure the Grants pay someone to replace it every week," she pointed out. "Any sign of the ghoul?"

I glanced over my shoulder, watching a few trees sway in the breeze. I saw students walking toward campus in the distance. The church was empty but a car passed by on the road every couple of minutes. The cemetery was still. We were the only ones present, as far as I could tell.

But my then my eyes darted to the woods.

"No. Maybe he's watching from the forest," I replied.

"In that case, we'll have time to make a run for it," Stevie said without a hint of fear. "He won't be able to leave the graveyard."

"How can you be so sure?"

"I've dealt with graveyard ghouls before," she admitted. "They're no big deal. Pretty sluggish. They're mostly just for scare."

"I had no idea you were such an expert," I said, still studying the patches of forest next to us.

"My Seer license is very much active, Ember." She brushed the detail etched into Muriel's resting place. "Also, I'm a medium. Cemeteries are like my second home."

"No need to explain." I held up my hands and took a step back. "You do your thing."

In the past, I'd watched Stevie use her gifts, and I'd admired her for it. But as we'd gotten older, it'd been difficult at times. To my knowledge, Stevie had never had problems controlling her gift. If anything, her gift worked *too* well most of the time. Seeing as she was one of the few psychics in the southern United States who could contact the dead, she'd been proud of her talents. She'd even added the symbol of the Clairs to her sleeve of tattoos.

"Muriel, you sassy lady," Stevie said. "Let's have a chat."

Stevie stared at the headstone and smiled.

"Is she talking?" I asked.

"Oh, yeah. I love her." Stevie held out her hand. "Do you want to see for yourself?"

"You can do that?" My heart raced. A progression of Stevie's talents was helping other blood relatives see what she saw. The fact that she could pull it off meant that there could be a spot for her in Lady Deja's council someday.

"Sort of," she admitted. "I've been practicing with Ma, and you might be able to see Muriel for a few minutes if you take my hand. It's hit or miss, though."

"Okay." A spark shot through me as I took her hand. The hairs on the back of my neck stood straight up, and my chest continued to pound as I stared at the same spot as Stevie. A faint glow appeared for a second but quickly disappeared.

"She says that her grandson doesn't have time to visit her anymore," Stevie stated. "And

Muriel agrees that Earle shouldn't insist that he be called *Dr. Grant.*" Stevie giggled. "Muriel, you're hilarious."

A slight glow appeared in front of me again, and I was able to make out mutters and soft whispers. The thought that I was hearing a dead woman made my stomach churn. I wasn't used to it the way Stevie was, and it felt strange to be in her shoes.

"Ask her about spell-blending," I reminded her.

"She can hear you," Stevie pointed out.

"Right." I cleared my throat. "Muriel, we're here on official Seer business, and we need to know what you know about spell-blending."

"Also, your kin weren't very helpful," Stevie added.

I clutched Stevie's hand tighter when the glow appeared again. It grew brighter and brighter, outlining the silhouette of a woman I'd been expecting to be an old lady. Muriel looked to be in her prime with flowing hair and a modest dress. And then the whispers were clearer.

Muriel was frustrated.

"It was a horrible display." Muriel stomped her foot. "It gave witches everywhere a bad name for decades. I *hate* talking about it."

"Muriel, anything you can tell us will help," Stevie pleaded. She spoke to Muriel as though she were as alive as I was. "So far, a young girl is missing, and another one is dead. We think there's an unregistered witch experimenting in our town, but we don't know who or why."

"But that's forbidden," Muriel shouted. "The last time it happened, several innocents died and all because of a love spell gone horribly wrong. The shifters even turned on us for a while. Lots of bad blood. Never use deer tongue unless you know what you're doing."

Stevie and I both looked at each other.

"What's wrong with deer tongue?" Stevie asked. "Is it worse than red pepper, because I can't get one of the victims to talk for the life of me."

"You can't reverse a red pepper binder," Muriel shouted, seemingly more frustrated. "And deer tongue is like magical gunpowder. It amplifies even the simplest of potions. Is this why you disturbed me? To make me relive all the horrible stories I heard as a child?"

Muriel's voice rang through one of my ears and the sound of rustling leaves toward the chapel shot through the other. I let go of Stevie's hand, and all at once, Muriel's image and voice disappeared. The sound of a *crunch* gave me goose bumps as I carefully searched for the source of the sound. I thought of the graveyard ghoul we'd been warned about, and just imagining the sight of sagging skin, sharp teeth, and bloodthirsty eyes made me cringe. I tapped Stevie's shoulder.

"Stevie," I muttered, my eyes fixated on the chapel. "Stevie, we may have company soon."

"Muriel says to hide behind a tree for a few minutes," Stevie replied. "Apparently, the ghoul they use isn't very bright."

Stevie and I walked briskly toward the forest. I kept my eyes on the chapel where I'd heard the sounds of rustling leaves and branches. As we found a thick oak to hide behind, the sound of another *crunch* rang through the cemetery. Stevie sighed, looking relieved that we'd managed to outwit the Grants' magical security guard.

I knelt down to wait in silence, and my foot hit a patch of rough thicket. I glanced behind me, and all at once my hands clenched into tight fists, and my torso froze. It was hard to take a breath, but I forced myself to out of urgency.

"Stevie," I whispered. I said nothing else. All I could do was point.

"What?" Stevie turned around and immediately her eyes went wide in fear. "Is that...?"

Hidden in the brush was a body—the remnants of one.

The flesh was almost purplish, and the rest of the corpse didn't resemble that of a human.

"Yep," I breathed. "That would be the ghoul."

"Can you kill something that's already dead?"

"Apparently, you can," I responded. "He looks pretty dead to me."

Chapter 14

The sky was gray and the evening air burned in my lungs as I stared at the remains of the Grants' graveyard ghoul. He'd been torn apart. Maybe eaten. And Stevie and I had no idea how or why. I forced myself to take deep breaths. It was time for us to leave. All we had to do was quietly run back the way we'd come, and everything would be okay.

I covered my mouth. I couldn't look at the scene in front of me anymore. The smell especially made me want to vomit. Stevie knelt down and examined the ghoul further. The fact that he was now a rotting corpse didn't seem to bother her as much. But a look of disgust was still apparent on her face.

I leaned against an oak tree to steady myself.

"The Grants sure know how to pick 'em," Stevie muttered. "He'll be okay."

"What?" I glared at her, wondering if she and I had seen the same thing.

"Yeah, once the Grants conjure his services again he'll regenerate," she explained. "At least, I think so."

"In the meantime, something bigger and badder wanted a snack," I commented.

Crunch.

The two of us stopped talking and leaned against the oak tree, studying each gravestone. The sound was still coming from the chapel. It was the same one I'd heard before, but I couldn't pinpoint the source. *Crunch.* A shadow appeared. It was short and round. It moved quickly to the nearest headstone and stayed hidden as the sky turned darker and the stars began to twinkle. It was waiting for the cover of night.

"Shoot," Stevie muttered as the shadow moved to another headstone.

I still couldn't see what the creature looked like.

"What is it?"

"Graveyard 101," Stevie whispered. "Now it all makes sense."

"Care to explain to those of us who don't spend quite as much time loitering in cemeteries?"

"It's a fleshbug," she stated. "This place must be infected."

"Excuse me?"

"The name should explain it all." Stevie narrowed her eyes as she studied the shadow, which had moved again. "That thing out there feeds on whatever it can find, including our ghoul friend over there."

"And us?"

"We're made of flesh, aren't we?" Stevie continued to study the fleshbug as it dashed from one corner of the cemetery to the next. "I have no idea why fleshbugs are attracted to graveyards. It makes absolutely no sense to me since most of the inhabitants have already decomposed."

"I expect that they enjoy the fresh ones then," I added, a little disgusted that I'd even said it out loud.

"True." Stevie tilted her head. "I mean, they're already dead so it's not like they'll go running off."

"I'm sure Mr. Ghoul tried to fight it off," I pointed out.

"Sure." Stevie shrugged. "He must have been extra dull if he couldn't escape a little fleshbug."

The thought did make sense, but I quickly realized that Stevie hadn't thought through a second scenario. I gulped, wondering how the two of us were going to get out of this one. Alive. My hands started shaking, and my heart pumped at rapid speed.

"There's more than one," I added quietly. "A lot more."

The woods looked as if they'd been hit with a miniature wind storm. Trees moved from side to side as small round shadows darted from tree to tree. There were more fleshbugs in the forest, and it was close to feeding time. No wonder the Grants' hired ghoul didn't stand a chance.

Did that mean that we didn't either?

Stevie cursed as she turned around and saw what I'd been staring at.

"This whole thing was a trap set up by the Grants," she said through her teeth. "Whether I'm alive or dead after tonight, I'm going to make those spellcasters pay."

"I doubt they know about the fleshbugs, Stevie. Muriel even said that they never visit her anymore."

"We're minutes away from being eaten alive, and you're defending them?" Stevie rolled her eyes.

"Whatever," I blurted out as the shadows grew closer. "You can yell at me later. How do we get rid of these things?" A bead of sweat trickled down my forehead, and heat radiated from my cheeks. My mind ran crazy, thinking through any bits of memories I had that might be able to help me.

"We send a written request to our regional representative who then hires an exterminator," Stevie recited.

"Be serious, Stevie."

The shadows moved even closer, and a fleshbug slowly rolled into the starlight emanating through the treetops. It was round and fat—the size of a small dog. Its skin looked tan and oily, and it had two beady eyes that fixated on the two of us. It reminded me of cockroach, if cockroaches were shaped like baseballs the size of Chihuahuas. It made me want to puke even more than seeing the scattered body parts of a graveyard ghoul.

Stevie cursed some more as she took a deep breath.

"Don't judge me for what I'm about to do," she shouted.

Stevie wrinkled her nose, hardly able to look down as she reached for a piece of rotting ghoul flesh. She let out a raspy scream as her fingers made contact with the corpse. Stevie hurled it as far into the woods as she could throw.

The fleshbug dashed after it like Yogi fetching a stick in the backyard.

"Please, let there be a place nearby where I can buy buckets of hand sanitizer," I muttered to myself.

I knew what I had to do. I had to follow Stevie's lead and help her distract the fleshbugs long enough for us to get out of there. I stopped myself from looking as I reached down, grabbed the ghoul's arm, and screamed as I threw it into the forest. Another group of fleshbugs chased after it. I held my breath for as long as I could as I reached down for another hunk of ghoul meat. This one felt soft and slimy. I gagged as I tossed it away from me.

"Grab a leg!" Stevie tossed bits of ghoul chunks even faster as more and more fleshbugs approached us. The sound of their grotesque rounded bodies zipping through the woods made it hard for me to hear my own thoughts. By the level of noise, I estimated that there could be hundreds of cockroach-like people-eaters lurking in the trees.

I did as Stevie said and grabbed the other ghoul leg.

Stevie briskly walked back into the cemetery, and another group of fleshbugs followed her. She tossed her ghoul leg, relieved to see all of them turn around and chase after it. But then another gang of them appeared just as quickly as the last bunch had disappeared.

I threw my ghoul leg in their direction.

"Run!" I yelled. My heart pounded, and more sweat poured down my forehead. Stevie and I ran at the same pace, dodging headstone after headstone as the sound of fleshbugs behind us grew more intense. My blood soared through my veins as I pumped my legs as fast as they could go. The side of my pencil skirt ripped, but I hardly cared. The rip helped me run faster.

The manicured lawn felt soft as my heels thudded against the ground. Out of the corner of my eye, I saw Stevie. She was deeply focused on the finish line. So focused that her foot caught the edge of a headstone and she toppled over. I screamed her name, realizing that any second her body would be overtaken with hungry fleshbugs.

And I had no bits of ghoul meat left.

Stevie cursed as she kicked away as many of the bloodthirsty parasites as she could. I panicked, trying to think of a solution, and an answer hit me. I grabbed the branch dangling near my face and used all of my weight to rip it off the nearest tree. It wasn't much, but it was better than nothing. I ran to Stevie's assistance and knocked a few away. They soared like baseballs into the distance.

Stevie jumped to her feet but fell over again when a fleshbug caught hold of her ankle. I kicked the nasty little thing, but it succeeded in sinking its gritty teeth into Stevie's calf. She screamed in pain and glared at the fleshbug with fire in her eyes.

I took my branch, carved it into my forearm until I saw blood, and then wiped as much of it as I could along the wood.

"You there!" I whistled, hoping the fleshbugs would exhibit even more doglike behavior. "Fetch!"

I threw the bloody stick as far as I could.

The fleshbug attempting to snack on Stevie's leg, along with some of its buddies, chased after it.

I exhaled, relieved that my plan had worked.

I clutched my bloody forearm as Stevie and I sprinted to the exit. Stevie limped over the short, brick barrier and I did my best to help her move faster. The moon lit up the sidewalk and part of campus. It appeared that the fleshbugs, like the Grants' hired ghoul, had been bound to the cemetery thanks to magical laws. Stevie and I didn't stop until we got into her car and locked the doors.

The two of us huffed as we sat there in a state of shock.

"Thanks," Stevie breathed.

"I don't know if I'll ever get my heart to slow down," I replied, taking deep breaths.

"We got lucky this time." She glanced down at the blood oozing from her wound. It was worse than mine, but her calf appeared to be intact.

"And all for nothing." I leaned my head back on the headrest and closed my eyes.

Stevie was silent for a moment.

"Well, not entirely," she explained. "Muriel finally started giving details when you let go of my hand."

"Yes, she looked younger than I thought she'd be."

"Were you expecting a talking corpse?" Stevie asked with a chuckle. "No, spirits that have moved on and choose to assist the living are all in their prime. Spirits that haven't moved on are the ones that look as they did before they died."

"Interesting," I commented.

"The ones that hang around the living get sort of stuck." Stevie shrugged. "Muriel had clearly moved on but was nice enough to assist with official Seer business."

"Too bad we didn't get long to talk with her."

"She did say one thing," Stevie said. "The spell-blending *incident* happened at night."

"So?"

"During a full moon," Stevie finished.

Chapter 15

I was done with Cottonberry.

It was late, and I'd run into the nearest drugstore for supplies—rubbing alcohol, glue, bandages, and Stevie's favorite candy bar. I'd driven us as far away from Cottonberry as I could, and I'd pulled over at the nearest motel. Luckily, I had enough cash for a room, and Stevie was wrecked enough that she didn't object to spending the night.

"Ugh, that hurts!" Stevie's leg twitched.

"What do you expect?" I responded, continuing to clean the bite on her calf. "Do you want me to kill all the little fleshbug germs or not?"

"Yes, but it still hurts." She closed her eyes and clenched her jaw as I wiped down her wound. The bite marks were prominent, and luckily the bleeding had slowed down. I wiped everything a second time before pinching closed the larger cuts and dabbing them with glue—a temporary fix.

"You'll have to see a healer when we get home," I said. "Who knows what a bite like this might do to you?"

"What about yours?" Stevie looked at the stains on my blouse. I'd bandaged up my cut, and that would probably be enough. "It's nothing. I'll get it looked at when we get back to Misty Key."

"What made you think of throwing the branch like that?"

"I don't know." I shrugged. "I guess I just figured they might be dumb enough to think it was another body part if I smeared some blood on it."

"I didn't know you had it in you." Stevie grinned.

"Hold that until the glue dries," I instructed her. I proceeded to doctor the rest of her bite. "We should get out of here as soon as we're all patched up," I said, changing my mind about spending the night. "The sooner we get back to Mom's, the sooner we can sort through all of this spell-blending nonsense."

"The full moon." Stevie sighed. "Maybe the shifters know something about this spell-blending *incident* too."

"Do fleshbugs live in the swamps as well?"

"Alligators do," she pointed out.

"Swell."

I finished cleaning and dressing Stevie's bite and then sat on the bed to rest for a few minutes. The drive back to the coast would put us there in the early hours of the morning. I watched as Stevie pulled out her cell phone. I held my forearm and tried to relax. I'd never been in such a dire situation, not even during my Seer training. Adrenaline pumping through my veins was all new to me. Strangely, it made me feel proud in a way. I'd survived, and now I knew what to do if I ever came across another horde of fleshbugs in the future.

"Ma wants us to get back as soon as we can," Stevie said. "She's informing Nova about the fleshbugs as we speak."

"Okay. Give me a few minutes, and I'll drive."

"You don't—"

"I *do* have to," I finished her sentence. "You shouldn't be moving your leg unless you want those holes to start bleeding again."

"You sound more and more psychic every day," she teased. "You're even finishing my sentences now."

"Like old times."

"Ember," Stevie said quietly. I opened my eyes and glanced in her direction. Her usual sarcastic tone had gone.

"What's the matter?"

Stevie cleared her throat and let a few seconds of solemn silence envelop the two of us. "Ember, I need to tell you something."

"Okay."

"Don't be mad," she added. Her expression was different than I was used to and for the first time in a long time, she let herself be vulnerable. No intimidating glare. No comments riddled with sarcasm. No tone of superiority.

In a way, it scared me.

"Just tell me. What's wrong?"

"That night at the bakery," she began, gently rubbing her bandaged calf. "I lied to you."

"Aqua? Is there something you're not telling me?" I sat up in hesitation.

"No, this isn't about Aqua," she stated. "It's about Dad."

I gulped, unsure if I wanted to launch into a discussion about my deceased father and the guilt I felt every day surrounding his death. The heavy breathing returned. My head pulsed with unwanted memories of that day and I tried not to look Stevie in the eyes. "What about Dad?"

"He never visits," she confessed, hanging her head. "I mean...he's never made contact with me."

"But you said—"

"I know what I said," she cut in. "I made you think I talked to his spirit all the time because I thought it would make you mad. The truth is that I haven't spoken to him since he passed."

"I don't understand," I replied. "Why wouldn't he want to make contact?"

"It's not like I haven't tried." She stared off at a spot on the wall. "But like I said, spirits that have moved on can choose not to talk to me. Dad has been silent ever since you left."

"And you're sure that he's moved on?"

"Positive," she answered. "It's pretty clear when a spirit is bound from talking like Dara's. Dad just doesn't want to make contact." She ran her fingers through her dark hair and let out a sigh. "I guess he isn't too happy with me. I wasn't exactly the easiest of daughters to raise."

"Stevie." I shook my head. "I'm sure his reasons have nothing to do with you."

"That's easy for you to say." She raised her voice, her usual tone returning. "You and him were like best buds. Maybe he'll talk now that you're back."

"Or maybe he wants *me* to talk first," I said, my heart racing. "Stevie, I—"

"Ahhh!" She clutched her calf and grimaced. "Okay, now that hurts like a mother! Something's really wrong here. I think I would like to see that healer now."

"Let's go." I wrapped my arm around her and helped her out of our motel room and into the car.

"My leg." Stevie stared up at the night sky, still hollering from the pain. "My leg."

"It's fine," I lied. "You're going to be just fine."

My confession would have to wait until later because Stevie's calf had swollen to the size of a tree trunk.

Chapter 16

"I had another dream."

My mother tugged at the moonstone hanging from her neck as Stevie screamed in the other room. Yogi jogged into the kitchen and joined in our conversation. We'd arrived in Misty Key about the same time as the healer Nova had contacted. Healers were hard to come by. Their gift was rare. As soon as the Clairs identified one, they fast-tracked them into training. A healer could read a person's energy—their life force. A healer could also set that life force back the way it was supposed to be.

"Was the dream about Aqua?" I guessed. The sound of Stevie cursing in the next room was pretty distracting. My mom sipped her morning coffee and tried to ignore it. She'd set Orion up in his room with a movie and headphones until it was time to go to school, which had been a wise decision on her part. Yogi sat at my feet, helping me feel a little calmer.

"The clock is dwindling down to nothing," she replied. "Her time is almost gone." She took another quick sip of her coffee. "You need to speak with Louie Stone."

"Why?"

"I don't know," Mom answered. "That's just what my dream told me. I saw the hunt, and I saw Louie. You have to go and talk to him before it's too late."

"I'll try anything." I took a deep breath, noticing that the shouting had stopped.

"All finished." A man about my age entered the kitchen with a smile. Yogi perked up. "She's a lucky one, but I managed to get all the venom out. She'll need to stay off of her feet for a few days."

"Not happening, Raymond," Stevie shouted from the other room.

"Keep her in bed if you can," he reiterated, paying little attention to Stevie's comments. I found it comical the way Stevie's shouting didn't seem to wipe the grin from his face. It was almost as if he couldn't hear her.

"Thank you, Raymond," my mom responded. She showed him to the door.

I took a deep breath as I approached Stevie. Yogi followed along behind me. Stevie was sitting on the couch with her leg up on the coffee table. Her calf was normal sized, and the bite marks had disappeared. But Stevie looked exhausted.

"I feel like my soul was ripped from my body and then shoved back in," she complained. "Remind me never to let Raymond come over again."

"He saved your life," I pointed out.

"So he did." Stevie laid her head back on a pillow and closed her eyes. "It's Wednesday, right? I have a special cupcake order being picked up today."

"I can help you with that." I placed my hands on my hips.

Stevie looked me up and down and all at once I realized that I hadn't changed my clothes. I'd driven to Misty Key as fast as I could go, all the while listening to Stevie moan and complain about her leg. Then I'd waited with Mom while Raymond had healed her bite. My blouse was still wrought with bloodstains, and my skirt was still ripped. I looked like a total mess.

"Not before you shower," Stevie informed me. "And let Ma handle all of the baking. I've seen you make toast."

"Speaking of Mom," I added. "She had another dream."

"Was it bad?" Stevie tried to sit up but quickly gave up as soon as her calf moved from its comfy position.

"We're running out of time, and she wants me to see Louie Stone," I replied.

"That old shifter?"

"That's right," I clarified. "He works at the hotel, and I'm wondering if he really might know something that can help us. You know, something about that spell-blending incident?"

"At this point, we've tried everything, and we should keep on trying." Stevie tried again to get up, but she grimaced when her foot hit the floor. "*Shoot.*"

"Give it some time," I said. "And some crutches."

"I can handle the bakery," said Mom. Yogi directed his attention elsewhere as my mom returned to the family room. He sniffed her feet before resting at my side. "Our customers will understand if we dial back our hours for a few days. I'd rather have my daughter back."

"I guess we can close," Stevie said as if her comment were an admission of defeat. "The only important thing is that cupcake order for this afternoon."

"I'll take care of that," Mom said. "Stevie, you stay here and recover. Ember, get to the Crystal Grande and talk to Louie."

* * *

Yogi escorted me all the way to the hotel. I fiddled with the rims of my glasses and hoped that the real Katie still hadn't shown her face. It felt weird to be going back, especially when my actual job back in NYC was on the cusp of collapse. I felt like I hadn't been to the hotel in such a long time after what had happened to Stevie and me in Cottonberry. Really, it had only been a couple of days, and word of Jonathon Carmichael's recovery had spread through town like a wildfire while Stevie and I had been away on official Seer business.

I kept my head down as I went through the back entrance. Yogi watched me go inside before turning around to return to the bakery. I forced a fake smile and happily walked toward an open locker in the employee break room. Someone grabbed my hand and pulled me into the kitchen.

"Luann?" I gasped as soon as I saw her face. Her eyes were the size of mini donuts as she pulled me into an open pantry for privacy.

"What are you still doing here?" she whispered. "You better get out of here before Mr. Brown sees you."

"Why?"

"Because the *real* Katie showed up this morning." Luann raised her eyebrows and glared at me.

"Oh, well—"

"Look, I don't know who you are or why you're here, but I thought I'd warn you," she interjected. "After the stuff we've been through, I figured I owed you at least that much." Her nervous glare quickly softened, and she sniffled. It didn't take me long to realize that she was holding back tears.

"Luann, it's not what you think, okay?"

"You don't have to explain," she responded, turning her head and wiping her cheek. "This is my thank-you for everything you've done for me. Now, get out of here. If I see you again, I'll have to report you to Mr. Brown so I don't lose my job."

It weighed heavily on my heart to see Luann so heartbroken. Again. She'd been through a lot—the loss of a friend, Jonathon's sickening attempt to seduce her, and, of course, Jonathon's accident. It was too much for one person to cope with in such a short amount of time. I bit the corner of my lip, wondering what to do. I had to waltz through the hotel like I worked there and I had to speak with Louie Stone as soon as possible.

"Luann." I sighed. "You're right. My name is not Katie. I came to the Crystal Grande with a bread delivery, and Magnus mistook me for someone else. I went along with it because I've been searching for information about my sister. Hunting for clues is more like it."

"Your sister?" Luann wiped another tear.

"Yes, Aqua. Aqua Greene is my sister." I took a deep breath, hoping my admission would help her see through my lies.

"You? Aqua?" Her eyes widened again as she took a second to process the news. A wave of relief washed over her face. "Oh, thank heavens. I thought you were some felon on the run." She wrapped her arms around me. "Here. Let me hug you. I thought there was something familiar about your eyes. This all makes sense now."

"Luann, I need to talk to Mr. Stone," I stated. "Do you know where he is?"

"Probably the gardens," she answered. "Although Mrs. Carmichael is throwing some sort of welcome home party for Jonathon on Friday night and the folks of Misty Key are all invited. She might have him setting up equipment in the ballroom."

"Luann, you're a lifesaver." I peeked out the door of the pantry. A cook and his assistants were busy preparing the food for the Carmichaels' big event. I crossed my fingers that I wouldn't run into Magnus Brown before I had the chance to get some answers. "How would you like to help me with one last thing?"

"If it's for Aqua, I'll do anything."

"Good." I gulped. "Because I'm going to need you to push me around in your cleaning cart."

After thirty minutes of hiding, scouting, and finally squishing into the bottom shelf of Luann's cleaning cart, I was on my way to finding Louie. I stayed still underneath a tablecloth as Luann wandered toward the ballroom. She wasn't allowed to push her cleaning cart around the main floor, and she'd received several scoldings from other staff members as she wheeled me toward my destination.

The cart stopped, and Luann nudged me with her foot. She was near the entrance to the ballroom, and I lifted up the tablecloth just enough to make out Louie and his assistant, Thad, hanging a sign in the corner of the room.

"If Mrs. Carmichael notices me I'm dead," Luann muttered. The sound of Mrs. Carmichael's voice boomed clear into the hallway as she complained that a few of the centerpieces weren't, in fact, centered.

"She won't," I whispered as I crawled out of the cart.

Luann wished me good luck and then quickly retreated toward the nearest elevator.

I took a deep breath and glanced into the ballroom a couple of times. My heart raced as a group of kitchen staff approached with empty dishes for the buffet, and I joined them as if I belonged. As long as I didn't stick out, Mrs. Carmichael would hardly know that I existed.

My opportune moment came when Thad excused himself and left the ballroom in search of a tool. I kept my head down as I walked toward Louie, grabbing his arm and whispering in his ear that I urgently needed to speak him. I then followed another group of kitchen staff out into the hallway. I opened the nearest door and stepped into the morning air. It was a relief to be out of the Crystal Grande without having the police called on me.

Waves rolled in and out of the shoreline and a couple of guests sat out on the patio enjoying their breakfast. It was another typical southern fall morning with a light breeze and full humidity. The sky was clearer and sunnier than it had been in Cottonberry.

"You'd better have a good excuse for coming back here," Louie muttered as he closed the door behind him. His gray ponytail looked shinier in the sun, but his leathery skin looked just as weathered. "Rumor has it that the manager informed the police department that an imposter has been traipsing around disguised as a maid. The real Katie is being questioned at the station right now. What a way to spend her first day in Misty Key."

"She has nothing to hide," I argued. "They'll send her right home."

"What news do you have?" He folded his arms and quickly looked over each of his shoulders.

"This is going to sound strange, but my mom said I needed to talk to you," I replied.

"What about?"

"Who knows?" I muttered, stamping my foot. "Okay, I don't know exactly what to ask, so I'm just going to start from the beginning. If you feel compelled to comment on anything for any reason, just do it."

"Spoken like a true Seer," he added.

"Okay, you already know that I suspect that a witch is behind my sister's disappearance, Dara's murder, and Jonathon's accident."

"Yes." He nodded. "And I haven't smelled any spellcasters around here, but you reek of them."

"I went to see the Grant family in Cottonberry," I admitted. "It turns out the supplies Aqua purchased from Gator could be used in a number of different spells. So that doesn't leave me much to go on."

"Okay." Louie nodded again.

"But Stevie and I did speak with one of their dead relatives." I paused for a minute. "Boy, that was a whirlwind." I debated in my head if the fleshbugs were worth mentioning. Just thinking about their beady little eyes and bloodthirsty stares made me nauseous. I decided against it. "I'd asked if maybe the ingredients I mentioned were being used to combine a few spells for whatever reason, and I learned that spell-blending had been outlawed by Wisteria, Inc."

"That much I know."

"The dead woman Stevie spoke to said that it all stems from a horrible incident that happened a really long time ago," I continued. "The only details we could gather were that innocent people died and it was the night of a full moon."

"Yes," Louie replied, doing his best to keep his voice down. "I don't know what happened either, but that's a condition in our treaty with Wisteria, Inc. You see, not long after that, Wisteria, Inc., tried to ban one of our long-standing traditions."

"Your full-moon hunt?" I guessed.

"The howl," he clarified. "To shifters of the wolf variety, howling at the full moon triggers the start of a new cycle within ourselves. We live in sync with the moon."

"They tried to ban you from *howling*?" I wrinkled my nose. "Am I hearing that right?"

"They claimed it was dangerous." He shrugged. "Apparently, the witch who'd accidentally killed all of those people used our howling to start some sort of magical reaction." He waved a hand. "The magic behind potion-making is still a mystery to me."

"So maybe this isn't about the full moon at all," I said out loud. "Maybe the witch just needed the howling from the hunt to do whatever it is that she's trying to do."

"Well, you can't bottle that stuff. You would need to be close to the swamps to hear us."

"And you can't be heard from town," I added. "I know that for a fact."

"Sounds like you *did* know what questions to ask." His eyes scanned the patio and shoreline. "Now, what will you do with all of this information?"

"What would you do?" I eagerly asked. To the residents of Misty Key, Louie Stone was just an old man who lived in a trailer outside of town. But to me, he was wiser than the community gave him credit for. He also wasn't fond of spellcasters, which meant that he had Stevie's stamp of approval.

"The only thing I know how to do," he commented. "How do you turn the prey into the predator?"

I shrugged. "You're the animal, not me."

Louie let out a raspy chuckle before answering his own question.

"It's simple. You set a trap."

Chapter 17

I hadn't thought about New York all day, or my job at Fillmore Media.

That was a first for me.

I'd returned home and had immediately relayed to Stevie the news about Wisteria, Inc. attempting to ban howling during the full moon hunt. She'd gotten right to work formulating a plan to catch the witch in question. In the meantime, Rickiah Pepper had stopped by with a pair of crutches and a gallon of her homemade peach sweet tea.

"Say what?" Rickiah had a hard time understanding why Stevie couldn't walk even though her leg appeared to be fine. No swelling. No bruises. No ghastly wounds.

"They're called fleshbugs," Stevie explained again. "You insist on knowing about all things magic, so try and keep up."

"Why would you go anywhere where something called a fleshbug exists?" Rickiah raised an eyebrow and refilled my cup of sweet tea.

"Obviously if we would have known they were there, we wouldn't have gone." Stevie held out a hand as if her logic were in plain sight.

A black curl fell over Rickiah's eyes, and she brushed it back as she thought some more about how Stevie and I could draw out Misty Key's unregistered spellcaster. We'd tossed around dozens of ideas involving a stakeout at Gator's drugstore, finding a way to reverse the binding spell on Dara's spirit, and asking the shifters to search the swamps for a secret bunker. All of our ideas had a shot at working, but we couldn't achieve all of them. At some point, we'd have to pick one, because we were running short on time.

"At work, we focus on the client," I began. Stevie narrowed her eyes as she gulped down more sweet tea. "What does the client want? What motivates them? What motivates their customer base?"

"Now that's fancy talk right there," Rickiah teased.

"I'm serious." I smiled, grateful that Rickiah was present. She had a way of pushing tension out of the room. "If we want to catch this witch, we have to dangle something she wants right in front of her."

"But we don't know what she wants," Stevie pointed out.

"We know she's making a potion, and possibly spell-blending," I went on. "Dara was found dead after the full moon, so we know whatever she's concocting requires the howling at the full moon like that incident from before we were born."

"You think this gal plans on killing a bunch more people?" Rickiah tilted her head, looking concerned.

"*Intend*, I don't know," I replied. "But we've been warned that what she's doing is dangerous. I guess anything can happen."

"Yikes." Rickiah shook her head. "Y'all better put your heads together and think of something."

"But the next full moon isn't for another few weeks," Stevie pointed out. "Aqua will be long gone by then."

An idea shot through my brain, and at first it seemed crazy.

"Unless..."

"Ember, there's no spell on Earth that can change the cycles of the moon," Stevie firmly stated. "And even if there were, you couldn't pay me enough to ask a spellcaster to perform it for us."

"No, but the shifters can howl any time they want," I commented. "Am I right?"

Stevie paused and leaned back in her seat. She didn't seem to object.

"Would they even do that?" Rickiah pointed out.

"They might if we asked them." I looked at Stevie, who nodded in approval. She gripped one of her crutches.

"So, they start howling, and our mystery witch scrambles to use whatever potion she's working on?" Stevie concluded. "I guess that could work. If anything, it'll confuse her, but how do we single her out?"

"Jonathon's welcome home party Friday night," I said. "The entire staff at the Crystal Grande and most of Misty Key will be there. The witch ought to be there too. When she hears the howling, she'll panic and probably leave the party."

"Or she could do nothing." Rickiah pursed her lips. "Sorry, someone's got to play the devil's advocate."

"That's true," Stevie agreed. "But if we set this up for Friday, that gives us tomorrow to prepare. Besides, what else are we supposed to do? Sit around and wait for Aqua's body to turn up?"

"I guess the last thing y'all need is another victim," Rickiah said. "Didn't you say Dara was a siren? So, doesn't that mean that this chick is targetin' magical folk?"

"Yes." I sighed. "But the witch will be wanting someone low key."

"That means I'm out," Stevie said. "All of Misty Key knows the Lunar Bakery and me. You need someone young and new in town."

"Like Ember?" Rickiah chuckled to herself.

"I said *young*," Stevie joked.

"I know someone." I held up a finger. "He's not a young twenty-something, but he is new in town."

"Is he hot?" Rickiah shrugged. "What? There's no harm in asking."

"That depends," I responded with a grin. "Are you a cat person or a dog person?"

Chapter 18

Wednesday night had come and gone in a flash. Stevie and I had fallen asleep right after dinner, the exhaustion having gotten to us. My mother and Orion had entertained themselves with a quiet night in and pizza, and Yogi had kept watch at the front door most of the night. We'd mapped out a plan for Jonathon Carmichael's welcome home party, and we had all of Thursday to gain alliances.

I sat at the kitchen table on Thursday morning staring at my inbox. Inwardly, I'd made my decision, but I couldn't find the strength to admit it out loud. My best shot at finding my little sister was tomorrow night, and tomorrow was the day that Mr. Fillmore would be naming a new Director of Finance. I wouldn't be there, which meant that all of my hard work was about to go unnoticed.

I tried to start an email to my boss explaining why I hadn't booked my plane ticket. I couldn't even start it, let alone finish it.

I quickly put my phone away as Stevie limped into the kitchen for her morning cup of coffee. I just hoped that when everything was over and I finally divulged the secret I'd been hiding, it would all have been worth it.

"Mom took Orion to school," I said. "And a sign is posted on the bakery door."

"Our customers won't be happy," Stevie muttered. "Are you ready for today?"

"Yes, but I can also walk like a normal person." I took a sip of my coffee and waited for a sarcastic reply.

"Today is better than yesterday," Stevie answered. "I expect that tomorrow my pain will practically be gone."

"Here's to hoping." I held up my mug.

I studied my map of the Crystal Grande's ballroom. There were two main exits and a backstage area that had been set up. One of the main exits was being used by the staff, and the other was for guests. If we could get the shifters' cooperation, we would have eyes on all exits as soon as the howling began.

And if he agreed, Thad would serve as bait.

A knock on the door made me flip my map over. Yogi let out a soft bark as he ran to the front door. Stevie began limping in that direction, and I stood up ahead of her. I swiftly left the kitchen before she had the chance. Yogi wagged his tail as I opened the door to Nova, our regional representative.

"I hope you've been expecting me," Nova stated.

"Not really." I forced a swallow. I knew she wanted my answer and she wanted it soon. "We were just preparing for a little meet-and-greet later on today."

"Yes, I saw that the bakery is closed," Nova said. Her reddish hair matched the color of her blazer. It was a bold choice of clothing for such a warm day, but it was also autumn. "Care to fill me in on your plans?"

"If we have to," I muttered.

"We do," Stevie called from the kitchen.

"Also, I thought you would like to know in person that an exterminator has taken care of that little infestation in the Cottonberry cemetery." Nova nodded.

"*Little?*" I repeated.

"Rest assured that the caretaker has been slapped with a fine for that one," she continued. "More people could have been injured."

"Or eaten," I murmured. Nova walked right past me and into the kitchen. I imagined that her Siamese ghost cat had a snide look on his or her face.

I flipped my map of the Crystal Grande ballroom back over. Stevie proceeded to tell Nova our plans to draw out the unregistered witch with some shifter cooperation. Nova raised her eyebrows and promptly tucked a fist under her chin, placing an elbow on the kitchen table.

"You know, all of this would be easier if you tried to hone in on your gifts." Nova looked at me, and her expression dug up flashes of our last conversation. I concluded that this was her way of helping me to see that my talent was useful enough to keep.

"I can try, Nova. But I'm not staking my sister's life on it." I avoided eye contact with anyone.

"If you focus, I know you can do it."

"Maybe in another life," I stated. "For now, I think I'll stick to something more likely to work."

Stevie offered Nova some coffee and pastries as I stared at my map for a while longer. It was only a cover. I'd thought through our plan several times, and I knew it by heart. Of course, with all of our suspects in the same room, the numbers could also point to the real killer. The numbers never lied.

But I wasn't confident that I'd be able to read them when the time came. They'd helped me when I'd found Dara's body and in Jonathon Carmichael's suite. But they hadn't helped me in the graveyard. How could I be certain that they would come to my aid at the welcome home party tomorrow night?

I couldn't be.

* * *

The clan of shifters that roamed Misty Key were part human and part wolf. Stevie and I approached their small community just outside of town. It was a maze of trailer homes near a local swamp—the perfect place for them to be themselves without too many onlookers. I'd visited the shifter community once as a kid. My dad took us. He was looking to hire a watchdog of sorts when he'd suspected a theft at the bakery. Louie volunteered, and from then on the shifters regarded the Greene family as friendly.

I kept a smile on my face as I glanced down at a wrinkly piece of paper. I'd written down Louie's address, and I'd rehearsed a speech over and over again in my head. I had no idea how he would react. Stevie limped next to me, using her crutches for balance. She'd complained about them all morning, and I was surprised she was still using them. But her leg was still sore.

"They can spot fear from a mile away," Stevie whispered.

"I'm not scared."

"Uncertainty?" she corrected herself.

"Well, it isn't every day that you ask an ancient species to change one of their longstanding traditions, is it?" I took a deep breath.

The evening sky was gray, and each trailer home provided its own unique pop of color. Some were new, and some of the homes had been parked on the lot since I was a child. A park with picnic tables and a basketball court sat in the middle of the community, and a few kids were outside playing.

The sound of their laughter helped ease my stomach.

We walked straight toward Louie's house, and as we inched our way deeper into the shifter community, I noticed something strange. A light breeze brushed past my cheek, and out of the corner of my eye, I saw that we were being followed. I gulped and nudged Stevie's arm. Her usual smirk quickly faded, confirming that I wasn't just seeing things.

By the time we reached Louie's trailer, it was as if the entire community were standing right behind us.

I knocked on Louie's door.

"No pressure or anything," Stevie whispered.

The door swung open, and Louie looked surprised to see me standing in front of him.

"Oh, it's you," he stated. He walked outside for a moment and waved his hand. "Seer business, everyone!"

The crowd behind us dispersed, and immediately I felt some weight lifted from my shoulders.

"What was that all about?" Stevie asked, an intimidating stare returning to her face.

"You two smell like spellcasters," Louie pointed out. He escorted us into his living room, which was also his kitchen, dining room, and bedroom.

"I shower every morning, Louie." Stevie helped herself to the comfiest-looking seat. "You make sure everybody knows that."

"The smell will fade with time," he explained. "There's little you can do to avoid it."

"But there is *something* that can be done," I chimed in. "I mean, how else would this witch be getting away with murder right under our noses—especially your nose, Louie?"

"She stopped Dara's spirit from talking, so I think it's safe to say she has thought of everything," Stevie said.

"Which brings us to the reason we're here." I took a seat next to Stevie and placed a hand on my chest. My heart pounded at a rapid rate, and there was little I could do to stop it. Aqua's life was at stake.

Aqua's safe return depended on Louie Stone.

"You're nervous," Louie stated. "That makes *me* nervous."

"Start with the disclaimer," Stevie said, crossing her arms. "Go on."

"I don't need coaching."

"You are my assistant," she snidely remarked.

I clenched my jaw and tried to focus.

"Okay, Louie, promise me that you won't form any sort of opinion until I've finished talking," I started. "What I'm about to ask of you is a big deal.

I understand that. Just remember that we are on official Seer business on behalf of the Clairs, and there are magical lives at stake."

"I promise," Louie agreed. The lines on his face creased as he studied me further.

"I know that you're well aware of the problem we're having in Misty Key," I explained. "There's an unregistered witch in town messing with forbidden magic, and so far, someone has gone missing and another is dead. There will be more to come. I hope you understand that."

"I do." Louie nodded.

So far, so good.

"We have a plan to catch this witch." I took a deep breath. The closer I got to the punch line, the more my stomach churned from the anxiety. "We think that whatever she's doing is dependent on the full-moon hunt—and more specifically, the howling."

"You mean like that incident a century ago?" He wrinkled his bushy eyebrows, a shade of gray that matched his ponytail.

"Exactly like that, except only one life has been lost so far," I confirmed. "The last time a witch spell-blended like this, a whole village wound up dead."

"Go on." Louie was on the edge of his seat now.

"We think she'll try again early if she hears the howling, and tomorrow night all the Crystal Grande staff plus most of the town will be at Jonathon Carmichael's welcome home party."

"Hell, she might even try and kill Jonathon again tomorrow night," Stevie added.

"Anyway." I took back control of the conversation. "We've arranged for people to be on the lookout at every exit. All we need is the distraction and the bait."

"I think I know what you're about to ask me, but I want you to spell it out." Louie's voice went hoarse the more suspicious he became.

"Is there any way you can orchestrate howling tomorrow night near the hotel?" I blurted out. "And we want to use Thad as bait. He's magical, and he's new in town."

Louie lifted his brows and clasped his hands in front of him. He exhaled loudly, and Stevie and I looked at each other. He bit the inside of his cheek as he pondered my request.

"Do you realize what you're asking?" he finally spoke.

"Yes."

"Howling out of turn has repercussions," he pointed out. "Only the elders such as myself would be able to do it without causing harm, and so close to town?"

"Just imagine the look on that witch's face when you do your thing," Stevie pointed out. "She'll go nuts at your expense. It'll be her undoing."

"Assuming that she caves under pressure," Louie argued.

"You saw how sloppy Jonathon's accident was," Stevie went on. "You know she'll cave under pressure. And we'll *all* be there watching."

"I'll have to discuss this with the others." Louie stood up, giving us his cue to leave. "It'll come to a vote."

"Thank you." I reached out to shake his hand, a gesture he reciprocated.

"As for Thaddeus," he added. "You'll have to ask him yourself if he wants to participate."

A door in the back creaked open, and Thad emerged with a lifted chin and tight jaw. His dark hair was gelled back, and a shadow of facial hair was apparent on his face. He wasn't wearing his usual hiking boots, but he still carried a smug look on his face.

"*This* is the new guy?" Stevie said quietly as if Thad couldn't hear her. "Nice."

"Stevie," I scolded her.

"Count me out," Thad stated. He shoved his hands in his pockets and pushed his way out the door. Stevie and Louie both looked at me.

"What?"

"Go talk to him," Stevie urged me.

"Can't you just make him cooperate, Louie?" It was worth a try.

"You know as well as me that I can't," he responded.

I braced myself for more resistance as I stepped back outside. My mind whirled with frustration as I glared at the back of Thad's head. I walked quickly to keep up with him, but it was hard in my usual pencil skirt. I'd run out of suitable clothes, and my business attire was my only option aside from borrowing one of Stevie's tank tops.

"My answer is still *no*," Thad said without even turning around.

"Now, hold on for just a minute," I demanded. "You haven't even let me explain."

Thad stopped suddenly.

"I heard everything," he stated. "And who put *you* in charge anyway?"

"You think I like running around town solving other people's problems?" I raised my voice. I couldn't help it. Thad had no idea what it was like to be me. "I have no choice in the matter. I'm like you. I was born with certain abilities, and that's just the way it is."

"Do you know who your parents are?" he questioned me. His sharp features weren't as harsh-looking when I moved closer to him.

"Well, yeah—"

"Then you're *not* like me, Ember," he stated. "I've gone my whole life not knowing what this thing inside of me was. I alienated myself from a lot of people. I've wandered around looking for answers my whole life. I've finally figured out what I am and you want me to risk all that for one of your little games?"

I frowned. "My sister might be dead if I don't do something."

"I'm sorry." He sighed, holding up his hands. "Look, I wish you the best of luck, but I want no part of this." He turned and continued walking.

I'd never met someone so guarded.

But even a man like Thad wanted something.

"Wait!" I yelled. *What does the client want? What motivates them?* "I can help you."

Thad stopped again and turned around.

"How?"

"I'm psychic, remember?" I stated. "If you help me out, I'll give you a reading."

"A reading?" His eyes wandered up and down my face searching for a catch. "You mean like with crystal balls and tarot cards?"

"Only the fakes do that," I informed him. "There is only one crystal ball that actually works and that resides with Lady Deja, the head of the Clairs."

"Forgive me if I don't follow." He folded his arms—his closed body language matching that of his attitude.

"Let me explain," I replied. "The Clairs represent psychics all over the world, and our mission is to act as mediators between the magical species. We're born with gifts that help us understand the conflict that exists inside everyone. When we turn twenty, we receive what we call a crest reading, and that tells us where our strengths lie and what talents we should focus on developing. Are you with me so far?"

"Sounds bogus, but so is the fact that I can shift into a wolf."

"We receive training, and we become Seers," I went on. "Part of our training involves readings. I'll read you and tell you everything you want to know about yourself if you help me."

"And if I'm dead?"

"You can haunt my sister Stevie," I said.

Chapter 19

I finally pressed *send*.

"Ready?" My mother wasn't doing so well. She'd spent the afternoon thinking through our plan after having another prophetic dream confirming that this was our only chance at finding Aqua.

"Yes," I replied. I watched my inbox, wondering how soon I would get an angry reply from my boss. Friday had come too fast, and I was still in Alabama.

That promotion wasn't going to me.

"Is everything else okay?" she asked.

"I hope so." I nodded. She already had enough to worry about, and my city troubles weren't much in comparison to the possibility of losing a daughter. Besides, I was pretty sure that she was one negative thought away from painting the front door black.

Yogi let out a soft bark as Stevie entered the kitchen with a smile.

"Ta-da!" She slowly turned, wearing dark jeans and a black top to match.

"Nice camo, Ma," Orion commented.

"No crutches," Stevie pointed out. She walked normally through the kitchen. She wrinkled her nose. "Okay, I'm not one hundred percent perfect, but I'm good enough."

"You look perfect for the swamps, but a cocktail party?" I questioned her choice of outfit. Although mine wasn't entirely appropriate either. I was wearing a T-shirt and jean shorts that I'd snagged from Stevie's wardrobe. It made little difference because I'd planned to find a maid's uniform so I could blend in with the staff.

"I'm guarding the backstage exit," she explained. "No one will see me anyway. Also, I don't want to be seen. Carmichael parties aren't my thing. Ma, do you have the stuff?"

"Use it wisely," she responded. My mom touched the moonstone around her neck and then gently took it off and handed it to Stevie. "All you need is a sprinkle, and he'll practically glow."

Jonathon Carmichael's homecoming party was starting soon, and we were set to meet the rest of the gang at the Crystal Grande. Rickiah and Nova were going to watch the main entrance, I was going watch the staff entryway, and Stevie was going to linger backstage. Louie Stone and a few select shifters were planning to howl at midnight as close to the hotel as they could without being seen, and Thad had agreed to hang out in the lobby alone. A sprinkle of my mother's moondust would broadcast to other magic folk that he was also magical. Moondust was used to amplify one's chi during particularly difficult readings. For magical creatures, it had a different effect.

"You be good." Stevie hugged Orion. She touched the back of his head and looked at him as if she were taking a mental picture of his face. "Listen to Granny, and always remember that I love you."

"I know, I know." Orion smiled, unaware of the dangers that awaited the both of us.

A killer witch was nothing to be casual about.

"You *will* bring Aqua back." My mother nodded with confidence. "I can feel it in my bones."

"Love you, Mom." I hugged her tight.

"Trust each other." My mother looked from me to Stevie. "You two are sisters. Nothing is more powerful than the blood bond you share."

"So you keep telling us," Stevie added to ease the heavy emotions cycling through the room.

"Have faith in yourself, Ember," she said quietly. "All will be well. Remember that."

"Thanks, Mom."

The glint in her eye reminded me of my father. He used to look at me that way too—like I could do anything I set my mind to.

The phone in the kitchen rang, and Stevie let out a yelp followed by a chuckle.

"Hello?" My mom answered it and immediately looked at me. "Why yes, she's right here."

She handed the phone to me, and I clasped the receiver a little tighter than normal.

"This is Ember."

A voice I didn't expect greeted me.

"There you are. I've been trying to get ahold of you all day."

"Gator?"

"Of course it's Gator," he responded. "Who else would it be?"

His deep southern accent and boisterous attitude didn't change when he was on the phone.

"What can I do for you?" I asked.

"I wanted to give you a heads-up about those numbers you gave me," he answered.

My mind jumped back to the day I'd visited him and looked through his black book of magical transactions. The numbers had spoken to me that day. And although I hadn't been able to interpret them, I'd written them down. I hadn't been much help in bringing Gator good fortune, but maybe he'd figured it out himself.

"Did you figure out what they mean?"

"They were numbers straight from my database just like you said." He chuckled. For a brief moment, I heard shouting in the background and then a whistle blowing. He had the TV on. "Bread and milk."

"Oh." I tilted my head and thought for a moment. "I guess that could mean just about anything."

"I know exactly what it means," he continued to brag. "They're for the bread and milk sandwiches." He chuckled louder this time.

"Gator, you've lost me."

"You know, the bread and milk sandwiches we folks make when a storm is coming."

"What do bread and milk have to do with the weather?" My brain ran for miles trying to interpret his logic. I came up with next to nothing.

"Oh, you're no fun. I guess I have to spell it out." He paused again, and I heard another whistle.

"Focus," I reminded him.

"Whenever folks catch wind of a storm headed our way, the first items we sell out of are bread and milk. People try to stock up, you see. So we always joke that folks make bread and milk sandwiches. Do you get it?"

"I do now," I said.

"So I've ordered an extra delivery of bread and milk, and I've raised prices by twenty-five cents," he stated proudly. "Folks are already trickling in. The weather station is predicting a pretty nasty rainstorm tonight."

"A storm?" I stamped my foot. "Are you sure?"

"Why else would you have given me those numbers?"

"Thanks, Gator," I responded. "And good luck."

"See. You ain't as bad as you think at this Seer stuff."

I took a deep breath. "We'll see about that."

I hung up the phone and wondered how the shifters felt about howling during a rainstorm. I hoped it wouldn't hinder our plans. My mom looked at me, and her eye twitched slightly. She'd been under an immense amount of stress seeing the things she'd seen in her dreams. I couldn't let her down. I had to give her hope.

"Is everything okay?" she asked. The tone of her voice was growing more and more fragile by the minute.

"Never better," I said with a smile. "And make sure you bring your herb garden inside. It's going to be a wet one tonight."

* * *

Storm clouds loomed overhead. It was a humid night, and the lights from the Crystal Grande sparkled in every direction. The hotel looked like a beacon sitting on the shore—magical and irresistible. A chill slithered up my spine as we walked around back and toward the employee entrance. I couldn't pretend I was Katie anymore, and I had to make it as long as I could without being noticed. I'd tried to wear my hair and makeup differently, but I wasn't sure if it would be enough.

As soon as Stevie and I stepped into the kitchen, I was confident that hiding my identity wouldn't be a problem.

The kitchen was alive and bustling with activity. Every cook on staff was attending to a pot on the stove or food warming in the oven. All of the waiters and waitresses came in and out, dropping off empty wine glasses and filling up new ones. The maids were handling the dishes and helping with utensils and linens. It was so chaotic that no one turned their head when we breezed through the common area. Stevie searched a laundry cart parked near the lockers and pulled out a wrinkled maid's uniform.

"You said you needed to blend in, right?" she muttered.

"It's dirty."

"You'll live." Stevie raised her eyebrows like my reaction was a test of my commitment to finding Aqua. I accepted the uniform, grateful that it didn't have stains or smell like sweat. Stevie waited as I threw the clothes on over my shorts and T-shirt. I had no problem blending in as long as Luann didn't notice me. She was the only one who knew who I really was, and I doubted that Magnus Brown even remembered what I looked like. He spoke to hundreds of staff and guests on a daily basis.

Also, he had so rarely looked at my face.

"Let's go." I followed Stevie as she exited the kitchen and nodded at Thad, who had been waiting for us in a nearby hallway.

"I feel like we need walkie-talkies or something," Stevie whispered, touching her ear. "All the pros do it."

Stevie eyed Thad, ignoring the confused look on his face. Thad was wearing a casual outfit unsuitable for work or for the Carmichael party being held in the ballroom. Stevie held out my mother's moonstone necklace and carefully twisted the stone until the tip of it came off. The moonstone was hollow, and about a teaspoon of shiny dust was housed inside for very special occasions. Stevie sprinkled a small amount on Thad's shoulder and smiled.

"What are you doing?" Thad protested.

"Relax. It's harmless." Stevie twisted the moonstone so that it was whole again and placed the necklace back in her pocket.

"Ember?" Thad glared at me. "This wasn't part of the deal."

"It's just a little dust," I explained. "Seers use it sometimes when they require extra help reading someone. It sort of softens your soul and lets a Seer see someone for who they truly are. But for magical folks, it displays their abilities. If our killer witch is in the hotel, she'll receive the message loud and clear that you're magical."

"And you'll be alone," Stevie added. "That's important too. Make sure you're completely alone. You have to be a convenient target."

"I'm starting to wonder why I agreed to this." He crossed his arms and leaned against the wall. "Okay, I'll stay right here and make sure I'm alone all night."

"And if someone approaches you?" Stevie tested him.

"I'll let them *kidnap* me." He shrugged. "Easy enough."

Stevie smirked and headed toward the ballroom, where the rest of our team was waiting. I stayed behind to give Stevie enough time to scan the next hallway, so we didn't run into Magnus or any of the Carmichaels. I checked my watch. The party was about to begin.

Thad glanced at me, and for a second, he forced a grin.

He looked even better when he smiled.

"Good luck," I said quietly.

"You too, Ember," he whispered back. "Despite what you may think, I really do hope this works."

I followed Stevie toward the staff entrance to the ballroom. Rickiah was waiting in an emerald green cocktail dress and bouncy, black curls. She clasped her hands in front of her when she saw us, and Stevie gave her one last rundown of what to expect. Rickiah had her phone ready and was prepared to take notes of everyone's comings and goings as soon as the howling began.

Our last team member joined us just as a man stood on stage with a microphone and started thanking everyone for attending. Nova was dressed in red—a color that suited her. She wished us all luck and quickly walked into the ballroom to mingle. Rickiah took a deep breath and went on her way.

"This is where we separate," Stevie said quietly, eyeing the stage. "But I'm not worried about you. You blend in even more than I expected you to. It's just your accent that needs work. You've lost most of it."

"I'll just keep my mouth shut," I replied, standing aside as a pair of waiters moved past us.

"Stay away from the Carmichaels," she reiterated. "The hotel manager lurks around them like a hyena. You don't want him to notice you or ask you any questions."

"I don't have a name tag, so that's a start," I pointed out.

"Let the howling commence." Stevie looked down at her watch, but when she looked up again her eyes went wide.

Stevie grabbed my arm and pulled me back toward the kitchen. I watched her in confusion, glancing over my shoulder every few seconds. I saw a flash of something shiny out of the corner of my eye. I knew what the problem was.

"*Shoot.*" Stevie kicked the wood trim in front of her. "This changes everything."

"Maybe they're here for the party?"

But I knew that Stevie was right. Our plans had been thwarted in a way we hadn't foreseen. Not only did I have to observe partygoers without being noticed, but I also couldn't enter the ballroom. It was too risky now. I could be hauled away before even getting the chance to sniff out the killer who had abducted my little sister.

And I owed it all to Detective Winter and the Misty Key Police Department.

"They're not here to eat, drink, and be merry," Stevie argued. "The police are here because they're looking for an imposter who called herself Katie, remember? They're looking for *you*, Ember."

Chapter 20

The crowd in the ballroom cheered and raised another glass to Jonathon Carmichael's good health. Jonathon sat in a VIP section away from the regular townsfolk. Jonathon's twin sister, Jewel, paraded through the crowd in a skimpy, nude-colored dress. The photographers from the *Misty Messenger* snapped as many photos as they could before her security guard informed them that there would be no more pictures for the evening.

As it neared midnight, the lights dimmed, and music had grown louder. The ballroom was packed with most of the locals and all of the hotel's current guests. Everyone had kept their places most of the night, including Thad, who was growing increasingly bored as he continuously pretended to text on his phone near the main lobby. I saw Rickiah and Nova, but Stevie was well concealed in the backstage area. Detective Winter and his men also had every exit covered, and they kept their eyes on the Carmichaels.

Mrs. Carmichael kept a wide smile on her face as she greeted guest after guest. She'd made a speech earlier in the evening about how grateful she was to have her son home from the hospital. She'd also mentioned that she would have given away all of her wealth just to have her Jonathon safe. It was ironic because Mrs. Carmichael was wearing a snug plum dress and a diamond necklace that was probably worth more than my family's bakery. She had diamond earrings that matched.

Magnus Brown had been glued to the buffet. He too greeted guest after guest, making sure that the food being served was up to par with Mrs. Carmichael's standards. She'd requested a rather elaborate menu—one that sent an array of smells through the hotel. A wide variety of local seafood from shrimp and grits to fried catfish let off steam in their serving dishes. Naturally, the kitchen had prepared every sort of southern comfort side to match. I'd heard whispers about golden hush puppies and creamy collards all night. The centerpiece of it all was the cake. It was a five-tiered hummingbird cake frosted with whipped buttercream and decorated with bunches of local wildflowers.

It was quite the feast, and it made my mouth water just seeing some of the leftovers being carted back to the kitchen. It brought back memories of countless family dinners. I'd missed the food I'd grown up with, and I hadn't even realized it.

Mrs. Carmichael hadn't eaten a thing all night.

From my quiet corner near the staff door, I had a clear view of her and Jonathon in the VIP section. Unfortunately, I had to leave my post every so often when one of Detective Winter's men got too close. I tensed when Mrs. Carmichael stood and approached the stage with a microphone.

It was almost midnight.

"I want to thank y'all again for coming out to the hotel this evening," she announced. "My son is alive and well thanks to good medical professionals." She glanced back and smiled at her son. Jonathon briefly touched his bandaged head. "A lot has been changing around here at the Crystal Grande. We're in the midst of some renovations, and we've been blessed with steady business. I want to take this moment to formally announce to the residents of Misty Key that the Carmichaels will no longer be the sole owners of this fine establishment. I have taken on a new business partner."

Gasps came from the crowd. The Carmichaels had owned the Crystal Grande Hotel since it had been built. Changes could be good for business, but not necessarily for the town. I scanned the crowd and saw a multitude of worried looks. A couple of guests began clapping and eventually the rest of the crowd broke out into applause.

"Thank you. Thank you." Mrs. Carmichael smiled and nodded. "Introductions will be made as soon as he arrives in the coming months. So, let's—"

A burst of thunder sounded overhead, and my heart pounded.

The lights dimmed for a quick second. The storm Gator had warned me about was approaching fast. I gulped, hearing the sound I'd been waiting to hear for hours. Howling filled the night. It grew louder, sounding like a pack of hungry wolves was headed straight for the hotel. With the added thunder, guests began to panic, and Mrs. Carmichael was at a loss for words. She hesitated on the stage and immediately looked at the nearest police officer.

"Not to worry." Mrs. Carmichael forced out a faint giggle. "We're indoors."

A guest near the exit covered his ears as another howl filled the night. The patter of rain against the windows added to the noise until the vibrations made the light fixtures shake. My muscles tensed, and so did everyone else's. My eyes stayed glued to staff doors. More howling filled the silence and whispers broke out into the crowd. They grew louder when Mrs. Carmichael dropped her microphone and instructed security to escort her and her children upstairs.

Before she could successfully leave the party, the lights flickered.

They came back on for a brief second, but then they went off again.

The ballroom was pitch-black.

A woman screamed.

The sound of shuffling footsteps echoed everywhere around me. The crowd seemed to be scrambling for some light and the nearest exit. Panic spread as people tried to find their way out in complete darkness. Several shoulders bumped mine, and someone even ran right into me. I pushed my way back down the hallway, trying to get to the lobby from memory. The halls were too crowded. Yelling and shouting filled my ears. With the power off, it felt impossible to find my friends.

Perhaps this was what the murderer had wanted?

The howling didn't stop, and neither did the thunder. The sound of pouring rain hit every window around me, and I began to feel claustrophobic. I placed a hand on my beating heart and tried to take deep breaths. I had to focus on my objective. Otherwise, our plans were all for nothing.

The lights finally switched back on.

Another scream echoed through the room. A crowd of people lined up in front of me, and all at once, the room broke out in whispers. I entered the ballroom, seeing police officers attempting to lead guests out into the hallway and main lobby. My eyes went wide when I finally realized where the screaming had been coming from.

Mrs. Carmichael let out bursts of sobs as she pointed and yelled at everyone around her.

Jonathon was unconscious on the floor. I gulped and covered my mouth. A tap on my shoulder made me jump, and I turned around to see Stevie. She bent over and caught her breath.

"Did you see anything?" she muttered.

"You mean apart from *that*?" I gestured toward Mrs. Carmichael as she stood and stomped from officer to officer.

"That way! She went that way, you idiots!" Mrs. Carmichael waved her hand toward the exit where just about every guest who had attended the party was trying to leave.

Stevie and I looked at each other.

"We have to find the others." I took a deep breath, pushing through group after group as fast as I could. It wasn't easy, but I looked straight ahead and kept my mouth shut. Stevie followed close behind and glanced down as I passed a police officer standing on a chair attempting to direct traffic. In my opinion, it made the atmosphere even tenser. I passed a woman hyperventilating in a corner. The man she was with fanned her face repeatedly. Groups of people crowded each window, staring in awe at the pouring rain as it flooded the streets buckets at a time.

Leaning against a wall near the lobby were Thad and Rickiah. I headed straight for them.

"She's here," I blurted out between breaths. "The witch is here, and she seems to have finished off Jonathon."

"Darn," Rickiah murmured as she pulled a bundle of shiny curls away from her face. "And Thad is still here."

"Thad, did you see anything?" I asked him. "*Anything* at all?"

"I heard the howling, and then the lights went out," Thad responded. His eyes darted toward the front doors. "When they came on again, I saw Luann run outside."

"In this weather?" Rickiah pursed her lips. "That girl is crazy."

"Oh, no." I rubbed my forehead, hoping it wasn't true. Mrs. Carmichael's screaming ran through my head. Luann had been present at Jonathon's first accident. She'd been with me in Jonathon's private suite, and she'd known Dara. "No. Please, let me be wrong."

"What is it?" Stevie asked, studying my expression. "Do you think it's Luann?"

"I don't know." I shook my head. "I hope not. She doesn't seem like a killer to me."

"They never do, honey," Rickiah said. "Speaking from what I've seen on TV."

"We have to find her then," Stevie firmly stated.

Nova bumped the side of my arm as she joined the group. Her cheeks were rosy, and strands of auburn hair had been knocked out of place. She clenched her jaw as she scanned the main lobby, looking annoyed at the manner in which most of the people around her were conducting themselves.

"Some people have a lot of nerve," Nova murmured. "I've been shoved more than once. Can you believe that?"

"Did you see anything?" I asked Nova, hoping that she'd have some information that would give us more of a lead.

"It appears the witch has struck again," she said. "And Mrs. Carmichael claims to have seen her."

"Luann." Stevie threw her hands in the air. "It has to be Luann. Ember, where would she have gone?"

"How am I supposed to know that?" My breathing quickened again as all eyes in the group fell on me. I felt like a hole was being burned into my skull, and I struggled for the right words. Logically, Luann being the mystery witch made some sense. But I still couldn't fathom how I'd missed it. Why was Luann in Misty Key and what was she up to? Her reactions to both Dara's death and Jonathon's accident had seemed genuine to me.

"Focus," Nova said. "What does your gut tell you?"

"I don't know." I shrugged. "Even if Luann was the witch, she could be anywhere by now."

"Can't you read the stars or something?" Thad asked.

"You shifters think you're hilarious sometimes." Stevie eyed him suspiciously.

"He's right." Nova cleared her throat to gather my full attention. "Use your talent. Tell us where she is."

"I told you," I argued. My stomach churned as the pressure to read the numbers consumed my mind. "My gifts don't work that way. They never have."

"They can if you—"

"Meditation isn't going to fix this one, Nova." I raised my voice, frustrated that she didn't understand. I'd worked hard at it. I'd listened to the Clairs' advice over and over again, but nothing had worked for me.

My gift had failed me at a time that I'd needed it most, and I couldn't shake the fact that it was about to fail me again.

"Then don't meditate," Nova suggested. She paused to collect her thoughts. A slight grin crossed her face, and I thought it strange that she'd stopped us all amidst a moment of mass chaos in order to give me a lesson I'd learned during the early days of my Seer training. "Be present in this moment. Think of the pandemonium. Another life has been taken.

Your sister is being held captive. You hold the key, Ember. You already know what to do next."

Nova stood in front of me and grabbed Stevie's hand. Before I knew it, my friends had formed a circle around me, shielding me from the rest of the world. I tried to focus on the numbers around me—the time, the main elevator, any sort of pattern in the décor. Like each time before, I quickly came up with nothing.

I watched guest after guest rush toward the nearest exit with a hint of fear in their eyes. I couldn't imagine what Aqua must have been going through. It pained me even to wonder, but the pain was enough to spark something inside me. Waves of memories flooded through my head and I let them take over for once.

I'd let myself down, and I was letting Aqua down.

A tear rolled down my cheek, and I quickly wiped it away. I closed my eyes to stop myself from crying. For so long I'd been over a thousand miles away and yet I'd come home only to discover that I was the same old Ember deep inside. I nodded, making peace with the realization that I might never be good enough. I was born a psychic, but that alone wasn't enough. I didn't know what was.

I opened my eyes to neon orange.

A pattern on the wall opposite me glowed, and I couldn't believe it. This time, the numbers had decided to spell it out loud and clear. *150 11000*. I knew it immediately. It was an address, and the street was one I'd driven many times. My dad had often used it as a shortcut from the main freeway to Misty Key's public beach. There wasn't much there by way of scenery, and I would have to look up the building number.

"Quick," I said loudly. "I have an address."

I relayed the numbers I'd seen and waited for someone to plug the coordinates into their phone. The circle broke as everyone fumbled to reach for their devices first. The numbers still glowed in my head. I didn't know what I'd done differently to see them this time. It very well could have been a spike in my emotions, as Nova had once put it. But whatever the reason, I knew the numbers were right.

"Yikes," Stevie muttered. "This can't be good."

"What?" I stared at her screen. The address was conveniently close to the shoreline and also near the swamps where the shifters carried out their monthly hunts during the full moon.

"This place has been closed for years," Stevie stated. "Why didn't we think of this before?" She hit her forehead with the palm of her hand.

"What's the problem?" Rickiah looked from me to Stevie. "If you know where Aqua is let's get moving."

"You can't come, Rickiah. I won't let you." Stevie glared in her direction, letting her know that she was dead serious.

"I'll go wherever I darn well please," Rickiah snapped back.

"It's the old shipyard," I clarified. "We went there once on a school field trip, remember?"

"Oh, I remember," Rickiah replied. "My uncle worked there doing boat repairs. He lost his job when they closed down and has been a pain in my mother's side ever since. That place is nasty."

"Well, that's where we're going," I responded. "Anyone who wants out, speak up now."

"Or *forever* hold your peace," Stevie finished.

Chapter 21

The howling had finally stopped, but the rain hadn't. The shipyard had long been closed, and the entrance was blocked by a tall chain-link fence. The four of us huddled underneath Nova's umbrella while Thad attempted to open the gates. He wasn't very successful, and after a few kicks he gave up and grunted as he shook the metal bars.

The rain was finally starting to calm down, but Thad was still soaked. His hair was sleek, and his shirt was damp. Nova commented more than once about the advantages of carrying around an umbrella, especially in a state where it rains a lot. Rickiah rolled her eyes and was the first one to climb the chain-link fence and hop over to the other side. I followed her, nearly losing my balance as my feet hit a mound of mud. Stevie was next, and she howled much like a shifter when she landed on her bad leg. Nova attempted to be proper as she climbed slowly, one chain link at a time. She also insisted on descending one step at a time instead of jumping down to save time. Thad was last, and he hopped over the fence like it was no problem.

"Why didn't you just do that before?" Stevie muttered. She narrowed her eyes as he strolled down the unkempt path with two sturdy legs. Stevie followed the group with a limp.

"How do we know what we're looking for?" Thad asked as we inched closer to a clearing of empty warehouses and rusting construction equipment.

"We don't," I said quietly. Raindrops rolled down my cheeks, and I covered my eyes to see my surroundings more clearly.

Nova hogged her umbrella and soon she was the only one under it. The five of us walked in separate directions, strangely drawn to different areas of the shipyard. I gulped as I glanced at the warehouses in front of me. There were several, and they all seemed like the perfect place to hold someone captive. I took a deep breath, noticing that every building and piece of equipment was marked by numbers.

I closed my eyes again and thought of Aqua.

"Over here!" Stevie waved a hand as she limped in another direction. "I know where to go."

I jogged toward Stevie as she hobbled deeper into the shipyard. Nova and Rickiah were behind me. Thad took his time, lingering near a stack of broken shipping containers. My heart pounded as I caught up to Stevie. Stevie was determined to keep her pace even though the discomfort of her injury had her scowling.

"What is it?" I asked, speed-walking beside her. "What did you see?"

"He's more of a *who* than a *what*." Stevie grinned through the pain. "He said that the blond woman is in warehouse thirteen."

"Warehouse thirteen," I repeated. "That's an easy guess. Are you sure—"

"The dead have no reason to lie," Stevie insisted. "And this guy has been here since the shipyards first opened. Milton was their first on-the-job casualty."

"That makes me feel a whole lot better," I muttered, my heart pounding as I saw the number thirteen in the distance.

Stevie stopped suddenly at the entrance. The sound of sobbing filled the night, and I couldn't tell where it was coming from. Stevie's eyes went wide as she looked at me. Nova and Rickiah glanced at each other from underneath Nova's umbrella, and Thad was nowhere to be found. I gulped, pointing toward the warehouse.

"I'll go first," I whispered. "The three of you walk around the perimeter and find another way inside. Our chances are better if we have her surrounded." I took a deep breath, but my heart rate was already beating at a rapid pace.

"Good luck," Stevie whispered back as she nudged Nova and Rickiah in the other direction.

I focused on the main entrance to warehouse number thirteen. The door was open, and the sound of sobbing grew louder in my ears. It sent shivers down my spine, and my stomach churned with fear. I had no clue what I would see on the other side of these walls—Luann, Aqua, a dead body. All I knew was that the killer witch was dangerous and she'd already taken a life.

Maybe two.

Hopefully, not three.

Darkness surrounded me as I stepped out of the moonlight. A light illuminated the corner of the warehouse, and the closer I walked toward it, the louder the sobbing became. A figure sat on the floor. I approached it with caution until I realized that it was, in fact, Luann. Her shoulders were slumped, and her face was buried in her hands as she continued to cry. Her hair was tangled, and her maid's uniform was covered in mud. She was a mess.

"Luann?" The sound of my own voice echoing through the warehouse gave me goose bumps. I clenched my hands into fists as Luann sniffled and looked up at me. Her eyes were puffy and full of tears. Her cheeks were rosy, and it was hard for me to discern if she was pleased to see me or not.

"Ember." She sniffled again. "You shouldn't have come."

"Luann." I gulped, keeping my distance. "Luann, why are you crying?"

"Is he dead?" she responded. Her hands moved to her tangled locks. "Do you know if he's dead or not?"

"Who?"

"Jonathon!" she shouted. Another rush of tears flooded her cheeks.

"I—I don't know," I answered honestly.

I watched in horror as Luann's fingers dug deep into her roots. She pulled at loose strands of hair as her sobbing turned into screaming. My eyes darted from her to every corner of the warehouse. It was too dark for me to tell if any of my friends were seeing what I was seeing. Luann was in pain, and she was beyond any sort of help I could offer.

But one thing picked at my brain more than anything else.

If Luann was *this* upset about Jonathon Carmichael, then why did she kill him?

"No!" Luann yanked out a clump of hair and stared at the tangled wad. "I never meant for this to happen. What am I going to do?"

"It's okay, Luann," I said calmly.

"What do I do?" Luann muttered, averting her eyes. "What do I do? What do I do?"

She continued muttering to herself as if she couldn't see me.

"She's about to suffer a psychotic break," a voice said from the darkness. "Such a shame."

"Huh?" I squinted, looking for the source, but I knew who it was.

"She'll be dead before the police can question her," the voice stated.

Footsteps grew closer, and soon I was face-to-face with the one person I hadn't expected to see.

"*You?*" I wrinkled my nose, having trouble picturing it. "*You* are responsible for all of this?"

"Warlocks are just as dangerous as witches, Ms. Greene," Magnus Brown replied. "Maybe even more so."

Chapter 22

My first thought after learning the identity of the real killer was that Stevie was right. Witches and warlocks couldn't be trusted. My fingernails dug deeper into the palms of my hands as I tightened my fists. My heart raced as a mixture of emotions flooded my mind and pumped through my veins like a shot of adrenaline. I wanted answers, but at the same time I wanted to punch Magnus in the face for all of the pain he'd caused my family.

"I expect you have lots of questions." Magnus clasped his hands together, still wearing the tailored suit he'd adorned at the Carmichaels' welcome home party. His eyes were darker than I remembered and his twisted smile suggested that he felt no remorse for his actions.

"Why?" It was the first thing that escaped my lips.

"You of all people should understand, *Ember*, that the magical community has no right to dictate the way we live our lives," he explained. "Yes, I know who you are." His expression was poised, just as it had been when we'd first met. He glanced down at Luann as she continued to cry and mutter to herself. "I'm going to put a stop to all that. I've found a way to level the playing field."

"Spell-blending," I murmured, remembering all of the trouble Stevie and I had gone through to acquire more information about the accident that had outlawed experimenting with potions all of those years ago.

"Yes, I've developed a spell that rips all powers from its host," he confessed, not the least bit worried that I knew the gist of his plan. My calves froze in place as the thought hit me. In my experience, there were two reasons that Magnus felt the need to brag about his accomplishments.

First, he wanted a colleague.

Or second, he was going to kill me anyway.

"And it actually works?" I replied as calmly as I could, deciding to play along with his delusions as long as possible.

"Almost," Magnus answered. He raised his voice so I could hear him over Luann's sobbing. "As you saw with Dara, I managed to strip her powers, but she didn't survive it."

"That makes sense," I said out loud. My stomach twisted itself into knots as I thought about my conversation with Dara's mother. Dara couldn't pass along her gift of song to the next siren in her family because she'd had no gift to give. And her spirit had been bound from talking about it. The whole thought made me nauseous, but I had to keep a straight face.

"Of course, I was going to let Aqua take the fall for everything, but I think I'll leave that to Luann. I could always use more magical test subjects."

"Aqua figured you out," I stated.

"She's smarter than she looks." Magnus chuckled. "I paid her handsomely to run my errands, but she still asked too many questions. I finally had to threaten her with shutting down the family bakery. Even then, I knew she wouldn't keep her mouth shut for long."

"So she's alive?"

"For now," Magnus replied.

I breathed a sigh of relief.

"No, Jonathon. No!" Luann's mania grew worse. She yanked out another clump of hair and screamed when she saw what she'd done. The entire scene put a smile on Magnus's face.

"Spells have side effects just like medications," Magnus explained. "Unfortunately, the hysteria won't stop."

"You made her *kill* Jonathon Carmichael?" I guessed.

"The chandelier was me," he responded. "The rest was a very powerful spell that I had some trouble with. I guess I'll find out tomorrow if he's actually dead this time. I wasn't aware of the relationship between Jonathon and Dara. He had his suspicions and threatened to turn me in." He pulled something shiny from his pocket, and my eyes widened when I saw my reflection in the blade. Magnus inched toward Luann with a kitchen knife.

I couldn't keep a straight face any longer.

"Stop!" I shouted. "What are you doing?"

"Relax." Magnus chuckled. He looked at me like a sideshow at the circus. "I'm not going to kill her. She'll do the work all by herself, Ember. She's gone insane, and there's no helping her."

"Put the knife down," I warned him.

"I would be happy to." He took a step closer to Luann, slowly bending down and placing the knife on the concrete right next to her.

"So, Luann kills herself and then what?" I blurted out. I failed at keeping my expressionless interview face for longer than ten minutes. "You're going to kill me too? And Aqua? And anyone who tries to stop you? Do you really want all of this blood on your hands? I'm sure you heard that things didn't end well for the last witch who tried to experiment like this."

"That witch was an imbecile," Magnus argued. His nostrils flared, and he raised his voice even louder. "She tested her silly love spell on an entire town without performing the proper testing first. I've made much more progress than she ever did. My power-stripping spell is much more advanced."

"So, you think stripping the heads of Wisteria, Inc., so that you can take charge is the answer." The fear that had been churning in my stomach turned to anger. I couldn't help but think about all of the innocent lives that would continue to be lost in the crossfire.

"It's not just that," Magnus said firmly. His gaze locked with mine. "Shouldn't you be free to choose if you even *want* to be part of the magical world? You should be able to have that normal life in New York City that you want so bad without ancient tradition getting in the way. I can fix all of that. This isn't just about power. *I* can make you normal."

"But the consequences—"

"I've worked out most of the kinks," he went on. "All I need is a couple more test subjects, and I'll have the potion polished and ready."

"But—"

"You can't deny that I have a point," he interrupted.

I gulped. Magnus was just as crazy as he'd made Luann, but he did have a point. That was the scary part. A potion that could take away my gift without any side effects would have solved all of my problems. It wasn't like I hadn't thought about it. For years, I'd been trying to shirk my Seer duties by building a new life for myself in New York City. My mother didn't understand, and neither did Stevie. But then again, their talents hadn't failed them miserably.

I took a deep breath. My eyes darted to Luann, who was still muttering nonsense to herself. She'd grabbed the kitchen knife, and an alarm went off in my head as she touched the sharp blade. I had to do something. I couldn't watch her do the unthinkable. In one swift movement, I dropped to the floor and snatched the blade from Luann. A sharp edge sliced through my own hand in the process.

I stumbled away from Luann and Magnus.

"You can come out now!" I shouted into the darkness, clutching the cut on my palm.

A deep burst of laughter filled the warehouse. Magnus walked toward me with his head cocked back as he laughed some more. My eyes desperately scanned every corner of the warehouse, but I saw nothing but shadows in the night. I gripped the handle of the kitchen knife—my only defense at the moment.

"They're not here," Magnus stated. "I'm no fool. I knew the moment the howling started at the party what you were trying to do. And *warehouse thirteen*?" He let out a hoarse chuckle. "Honey, it was all a setup."

"Where are they?" I said through my teeth.

"You would be surprised how many of these old machines still work," he pointed out. "Do you see that giant crane outside? Your friends are tied up in that shipping container hanging from the very top."

"But how?"

"Magic." He shrugged. "Go ahead and try to save them." He covered his mouth to hold back more laughter. He looked at his watch. "The crane will drop them in about five minutes. You'll die trying to stop it."

The numbers swarmed every thought in my head as I sprinted out of the warehouse and searched the night sky for anything resembling a crane. Part of me hoped that Magnus had been bluffing, but my heart sank when I saw exactly what he'd described. In the middle of the old shipyard, the long arm of a crane dangled a single shipping container hundreds of feet in the air. As I ran closer to it, I heard shouting.

"It's a lattice boom."

I jumped when I saw Thad standing beside me, and he dodged out of my way.

"For the love of sweet tea, Thad. Can't you see I'm holding a knife?"

"The type of crane," he pointed out, eyeing my knife. "See those ropes? They go through—"

"I'm not interested in that," I blurted out. "How do I get them down?" I glanced over my shoulder. "And how did you get here?"

"Louie says I should follow my instincts, and I caught a whiff of something," Thad responded. "I think I know where your sister is."

"You do?" My eyes went wide, and my heart pounded with so much joy that I could have kissed him.

"You can thank me later." Thad crossed his arms and stared up into the sky. "They're not up there."

I watched as the shipping container dangled from side to side. More shouting filled the night, and I searched every bit of my brain for a solution to my problem.

"Don't you hear them?" I asked.

"I hear something, but they're not up there." Thad nodded. "I would've smelled it."

"And I'm just supposed to trust you?" I said, the panic swirling inside of me.

"No offense but your sister, Stevie, smells like sourdough. I'm positive that they're not up there."

"But—" My chest went tight as the shipping container shook some more. I ran to the machine, hoping that I could find a way to turn it on and set the shipping container down myself.

Thad let out a yelp as the container swung again and dropped to the ground below. My lungs practically shattered along with it. A loud *boom* pierced the night, and I instinctively ran toward the scene, terrified that I would find my sister in a bloody heap.

But I found nothing but broken materials.

"I told you." Thad walked off, and I followed him. As soon as he realized I was right behind him, he broke out into a run.

Thad ran past the entrance and to the opposite end of the shipyard. Another cluster of warehouses awaited us and I opened my eyes wider in disbelief as one of the numbers glowed from afar. It was the one Thad ran toward, and as soon as we reached our destination, I stopped to catch my breath. Thad wasted no time kicking in the door so we could run inside. I held the kitchen knife in one hand and braced myself for whatever was ahead.

I saw a light.

I saw Stevie.

And more importantly, I saw my kid sister, Aqua.

A tear rolled down my cheek

"Ember." Thad cleared his throat and nudged my shoulder.

Stevie, Nova, and Rickiah were all tied up next to Aqua. Stevie looked more annoyed than anything else. I ran for the ropes and cut Stevie free with my knife. Stevie glanced down at the blade, impressed. I ran to Aqua next. Studying her facial features was almost like looking in a mirror, especially now that she was older. Her complexion was pale, and her cheeks were sunken in like she hadn't had a proper meal in a long time.

"And the games continue." Magnus appeared, and Thad growled like Yogi did when he was upset. Magnus clapped his hands before grabbing Stevie around the neck. This time he had a handgun, and he pointed it directly at Stevie as she squirmed. "Obviously, I'm not going to let more test subjects go to waste. I need all of the magical volunteers I can get."

"Of course, he goes for the gimp," Stevie replied. "And did he really just call us *volunteers*?" Even with a gun pointed to her head, Stevie never feared to speak her mind.

"The manager of the Crystal Grande," Nova stated. "Now, I've seen everything."

"*That suit*," Rickiah pointed out, shooting him a disappointed look. "Now, *I've* seen everything."

"Let me just remind everyone that *I* have the gun," Magnus responded. "*Me*. Y'all would do well to listen to me." A bead of sweat trickled down his face. He waved his gun in the air, and the moment he did, an odd breeze drifted through the room.

Out of the corner of my eye, I saw something I had trouble comprehending. The change was instant, and standing next to me, on all fours, was a dark-haired wolf with hungry, ice-like eyes. My entire body froze as it bared teeth that looked sharper than my kitchen knife. Magnus's eyes went wide as he pointed his gun at the creature.

But it was too late.

The wolf leaped on top of Magnus, and I ran for Stevie. I grabbed her wrist and pulled her to the floor. A shot fired as Magnus fell. I pushed Stevie away from the chaos and felt a sharp pain in my side. I looked down and saw a stain of crimson on my hand. It wasn't my cut.

I'd been shot.

"Hang in there, Ember," Stevie said over the sound of Magnus shouting. "And whatever you do, don't look to your right."

My eyelids felt heavy, and all I could think about was letting my family down. Again. My memories jumped back to the cool summer night when I sat alone with my dad in the kitchen. He'd been reading the *Misty Messenger,* and I'd been complaining about the way Stevie left candy wrappers in the bag instead of throwing them all in the trash.

"Stevie." The words were hard to utter, and it was increasingly difficult to keep my eyes open. I used every ounce of energy I had left to focus. "Stevie, don't hate me."

"What do you mean, Ems?" She rubbed the side of my cheek. "Just hang in there. You'll be all right."

"It was my fault," I confessed. That night consumed my thoughts. It played over and over again in my head. "Dad died because of me."

"What?" Stevie glared at me the way she usually did, and I prayed that she wasn't looking at me that way because I was already dead.

Dead or alive, the guilt wasn't gone.

"The numbers spoke to me that night, but I didn't listen." I closed my eyes for a second and saw myself back in my parents' kitchen. My dad had set the *Misty Messenger* down on the table, and several letters and numbers had jumped out at me. I'd had a stressful day at the bakery, so I'd ignored them. I'd left the kitchen, and when I'd returned, my dad had been out cold.

That issue of the *Misty Messenger* had forever haunted my dreams ever since.

A warning had been spelled out for me, and I hadn't noticed. I could've called an ambulance. I could've been there when it happened. My father could still be alive if it weren't for my carelessness.

"Ember, hello? Stay with me."

I opened my eyes and saw Stevie's face.

"I knew about the heart attack," I said again. "It was right there in the paper Dad was reading.

He's dead because of me. He won't speak to you because of me."

"Calm down, sis."

My eyes closed again, and this time they stayed closed.

Chapter 23

"Swipe down. No, not up. Swipe *down*."

I looked around, unsure of what I was seeing. I was in a plain white room. Bouquets of flowers and balloons filled my bedside table. Yogi perked up and wagged his tail when I moved my head. Orion sat at the edge of my bed with his nose in a comic book. My mom and two sisters sat in chairs right next to me. My mom was asleep, and Stevie and Aqua were doing something on Aqua's phone.

"I swiped down," Stevie argued.

"No, you swiped up," Aqua replied. "Now Brandon from Cottonberry is going to think I'm into him."

"I don't get this app." Stevie frowned.

Yogi leaped up on my bed, and a sharp burst of pain erupted through my side as I tried to pet him.

"Ow," I gasped. I noticed my bandage and the IV hooked to my arm.

"Well, it's about time you woke up." Stevie smiled, and Aqua put her phone away.

"Aqua, you're safe," I said.

"All thanks to you," she replied. Her hair was long and a caramel color that was similar to mine. Her cheeks were rosy, and she looked as if she'd returned to her usual self.

"How did I get here?" My memories of the shipyard were fuzzy, but I did remember one thing. I remembered what I'd said to Stevie. I was confused by the fact that she was still speaking to me. Either she hadn't understood my confession about our dad, or she was just being nice to me until I healed.

"You almost died," Orion commented as if the statement were a compliment. "The nurse changed your bandage, and it was covered in blood. Also, that machine over there is supposed to sound an alarm if your heart stops beating."

"Yes, you were shot," Stevie clarified, waving at Orion to stop talking. "Magnus has been delivered to the police and your name has been cleared with Detective Winter thanks to Nova and the Clairs."

"You mean what's left of Magnus," Orion muttered with a smirk.

"Magnus is alive enough to pay for his crimes." Stevie pointed a finger at her son. "And what did I tell you about eavesdropping on my calls?"

"Oh, darling." My mother opened her eyes and smiled as she touched my shoulder. "You're awake. How are you feeling?"

"Strange," I admitted. "But alive." I stared at Stevie. "I am alive, right?"

"Very," she responded. Stevie reached into her pocket and handed me my cell phone. "I grabbed this from your room. I thought you might need it."

I looked at my screen and saw that I had several missed calls.

All from the office.

"*Shoot*," I muttered. "My boss isn't too happy with me."

"We'll give you some privacy," my mom chimed in. "Come on, girls, let's head down to the cafeteria." She stood up and grabbed Orion's hand.

"I'm a boy, Granny," Orion said.

"You're a lovely young man," my mom responded.

Aqua giggled and held open the door. Stevie followed right behind them.

"Hang on, Stevie," I called to her.

"If you need groveling advice, I'm not really the gal for that," Stevie stated. "Although gunshot wound is a pretty good excuse for missing a full week of work."

"That doesn't matter." I tossed my phone aside. "Back in the warehouse, I said some things."

"Oh, that." Stevie nodded and took a deep breath.

"So, you heard what I said?"

"Yeah, I did." Stevie's expression softened, and she gently patted Yogi on the head. "Is that why you've been gone all this time? You thought Dad's heart attack was *your* fault?"

"The signs were all there," I said quietly. "I'm just not Seer material, Stevie. I didn't know how else to get away from magic."

"Well, for what it's worth, I'm not mad."

"Don't be nice to me just because I got shot," I argued.

"I have no problem being straight with you," she pointed out. "And because of you, Aqua is alive and so am I. Let's call it even."

She held out her hand.

"Truce," I said, accepting the notion.

"Truce."

* * *

I had déjà vu when Nova walked through the doors of the bakery and cut through the long line at the register. I'd only been home from the hospital for a day, and already I'd received an outpouring of friendly gestures. Unfortunately, my boss, Mr. Cohen, had thought differently. Another week had passed, and I was still in Alabama. As predicted, I'd been passed over for a promotion and part of me wondered if I had a job anymore at all. I'd taken a short leave of absence, and my boss hadn't been happy about it. A gunshot wound didn't seem to sway his way of thinking either.

"There you are." Nova sat down across from me. I took a sip of my morning coffee and a bite of my cranberry scone. I'd felt more relaxed the past few days than I had at our corporate retreat in the Hamptons last year. That was mostly because Stevie didn't hate me, Aqua was safe, and my guilt had finally loosened its hold over me.

"Yes," I replied. "I'm still in Misty Key."

"Good." Nova placed a packet of papers in front of me. "It's all done. All you have to do is sign right here, and your Seer license is renewed." She flipped to the first page and pointed to a signature line.

"Just like that?"

"Well, I do suggest you brush up a little, but I think you've proven that you can handle yourself in the field." Nova cleared her throat and produced a fiery red pen that matched the shade of her bun.

"Thank you, Nova. Thank you for clearing everything up with the police and helping me find my sister."

"But?" Nova raised her eyebrows.

"But I still can't guarantee anything," I responded. "I know my gift has a lot of potential but I have no idea why it suddenly worked at the hotel and won't work now, for example."

"What did you do differently that night?" Nova paused and waited for me to think through those moments very carefully.

"I thought about my sister," I admitted. "About my family and how I didn't want to let them down."

"There you go." Nova snapped her fingers as if the answer were sitting right in front of me.

"Are you saying my talent works when I feel sorry for myself?"

"No," she protested. "I'm saying that it works when you embrace the psychic within."

"Nova." I rolled my eyes.

"You're finally starting to accept yourself for who you really are," Nova said plainly. "A southern gal. A psychic. A sister and auntie."

"I guess I sort of see your point." I had to admit that coming face-to-face with my past hadn't been easy, but it had brought me inner peace.

"Good. Sign the paper."

"One more thing," I added. "I heard that Jonathon Carmichael is alive, but what about Luann?"

"Mrs. Carmichael's memory of that night has been blurred," Nova reported. "We've done all we can to help Luann, but I'm afraid a part of her soul will always be a bit frazzled by what happened. I'm looking for a suitable place for her to start over. She shouldn't be near the Carmichaels anymore."

"She can work here," Stevie chimed in as she joined us at the table. She took a deep breath and sipped a tall glass of sweet tea while Aqua took her place at the register. "Yeah. Ember has been looking through our books, and it turns out that we can afford to hire an employee."

"Is that right?" Nova glanced at me. "I guess I could approve that kind of request if I knew that Luann would have sufficient supervision." Her gaze slipped to the papers sitting in front of me.

I smiled and picked up her pen. Luann deserved a second chance just like the rest of us. And who was I to deny her that? I didn't know what that meant for my job and tiny apartment back in NYC, but I couldn't keep running from who I truly was. I pressed firmly on the form as I signed my name.

I was Ember Greene, southern gal and psychic sister.

"There," I stated. "Now, you can stop sending me letters."

"No need." Nova stood up. "We're plenty busy, so you should rest up for your next big case."

"No more witches, please," Stevie muttered.

Nova giggled as she put away her papers and put on a fresh coat of lip gloss. "How do you feel about vampires?"

Lunar Bakery Wheat Bread

It's outta this world

2 ½ cups warm water (warmest tap water will usually do)
1 ½ tablespoons yeast
4 cups whole wheat flour
3 – 4 cups all-purpose flour
1/3 cup vegetable oil
1/3 cup honey
2 ½ teaspoons salt
1-2 tablespoons vegetable oil for kneading

Instructions

Add warm water and yeast in mixing bowl, add 2 cups of wheat flour and gently mix until combined. Place kitchen towel over bowl and place in enclosed area (microwave works well). Set timer for 15 minutes.

When the yeast-flour-water mixture is ready, add oil, honey and salt, and then mix until combined.

Begin adding the rest of the flour (both wheat and white) one cup at a time. Start kneading once the dough becomes stiff. Continue kneading until the dough is no longer sticky. Pour oil for kneading onto a clean surface and begin kneading the oil into the dough. When the dough is no longer floury and has a smooth surface, you are ready to move on to the next step.

Spray two bread pans with non-stick spray, and pre-heat the oven to lowest temperature setting (mine is about 170°F). When the oven reaches temperature turn it off, and allow some of the heat to escape. Separate dough into two equal sized loafs and place in loaf pan, press down to fill the pans. Cover both loafs with a kitchen towel and place in the warm oven. Set the timer for 45 minutes. When the timer goes off, gently remove the risen loafs and place to the side, heat the oven to 350°F.

When the oven is to temperature, gently remove the kitchen towels, careful not to touch the dough (it will deflate if you handle it). Bake for 45 minutes until the loaves have browned.

Enjoy!

Acknowledgements

A special thanks to the friendly folks of Montgomery, Alabama. You know who you are. Thanks for you kindness and hospitality.

Thanks Joe for letting me use your secret bread recipe.

Thanks Christine, Ashley, and Annie.

Thanks to all of my readers. I wouldn't be here without you.

Books by A.GARDNER

Bison Creek Mysteries:

Powdered Murder

Iced Spy

Frosted Bait

Poppy Peters Mysteries:

Southern Peach Pie And A Dead Guy

Chocolate Macaroons And A Dead Groom

Bananas Foster And A Dead Mobster

Strawberry Tartlets And A Dead Starlet

Wedding Soufflé And A Dead Valet

Ice Cream Bombes And Stolen Thongs (short story
in the "Killer Beach Reads" collection)

Thanks, Y'all!

To be notified of sales and new releases, sign-up for my author newsletter at **www.gardnerbooks.com** where I post fun extras. Learn more about me and what I'm working on by following me on social media:

Facebook: @gardnerbooks

Instagram: @agardnerbooks

Twitter: @agardnerbooks

Made in the USA
San Bernardino, CA
17 September 2018